PEPPERMINT CHOCOLATE MURDER

A MAPLE HILLS COZY MYSTERY #2

WENDY MEADOWS

MAJESTIC OWL PUBLISHING LLC

1

The Elk Horn Lodge stood sixteen miles northeast of town. It sat next to a lake, its shore lined with canoes, rowboats and paddle boats. Large, healthy and lush trees surrounded the lodge and lake like a loving mother holding her children tightly against her bosom. Having never been to the lodge before, Nikki couldn't believe how incredibly beautiful the landscape was; the trees were much more verdant and thick than those in her own yard. It seemed to her, as Hawk tugged his jeep off a narrow, two-lane back road onto a long dirt driveway leading down to the lodge, as if the entire world had changed right before her eyes. "It's so beautiful."

"The lodge sits only three miles from the Canadian border," Hawk explained, easing the jeep down the driveway. "The lodge is owned by Mr. and Mrs. Snowfield. I don't know that much about them except that they built it in 1978 and have been here ever since."

Nikki spotted the lake, sparkling like diamonds through

a set of thick trees. Then she noticed a lot of vehicles. It was tourist season, after all, and all of the hotels in town were booked solid. "Is this lodge very popular?" she asked Hawk.

Hawk shrugged his shoulders. "I can't really say," he answered, glancing at Nikki. "Listen, Pop isn't going to like you being here. You're not going to get first dibs on this case, okay? At best, you're going to get some leftovers. I'll give you whatever information I can."

Nikki understood. She appreciated Hawk being honest with her. Reaching her left hand out, she examined his damp shirt. "I won't be any trouble, partner."

Hawk sighed and then grinned. He liked Nikki, but having her partner with him on cases sure was going to cause him some grief. Spotting Chief Daily's car parked in front of a log cabin that served as a lobby, Hawk brought the jeep to a stop. "Okay," he said, "get out and stay out of sight for now. Walk down to the lake. I'll come and get you when the coast is clear."

"In other words, when Chief Daily leaves," Nikki told Hawk. "I understand."

"Listen," Hawk turned to Nikki, "Pop and I, well, we're getting to know each other, but the ground we're on isn't exactly stable, you know. I admit I don't make it too easy on Pop, and he returns the favor often enough. If he sees you here, well, the sky just might fall. For now, you're my silent partner."

"You got it." Nikki smiled at Hawk. Opening the door, she got out and quickly jogged between a set of trees and disappeared. Hawk watched her vanish into the trees and then drove up to the lobby.

Peering out from behind a tree, Nikki watched Hawk park next to Chief Daily's car and then get out. She counted two police cars, a coroner's car and a brown Wagoneer, all parked in front. Behind the lobby stood the lodge, sitting like a cozy dream waiting to be entered. The lodge was a large, long, two-story wooden building that suggested nights filled with cozy fires and hot chocolate. Even though the weather was warm, she envisioned the lodge covered with snow, people out on skis, kids ice skating on the lake. "But where are the people?" she asked herself, spotting only a single white BMW parked at the side of the lodge.

Watching Hawk glance in her direction, Nikki stayed out of sight until he opened the front door of the lobby and vanished inside. Wanting to make a dash to the BMW to get the license plate number, Nikki bit down on her lower lip. If she was seen by anyone, that would be all she wrote for her. It seemed that everyone was in the lobby area. Nikki searched the lodge but couldn't see a single person. "If I'm fast…" she said, taking a daring chance.

Exploding out from behind the tree she was hiding behind, Nikki ran at an angle across the warm grass toward the white BMW. Feeling her feet leave the grass and hit gravel, she picked up her speed. Looking toward the lobby, she ran to the BMW, slid to a stop, read the license plate number, and then, like lightning, disappeared back into the trees just as Chief Daily walked out of the lobby. Breathing hard, she eased her head out from behind a tree and watched. A tall, thin man with a plump belly followed Chief Daily out of the lobby. Nikki listened.

"Take the body to the morgue," Chief Daily told the man, "after my son takes a look around. I'll be back in town."

"Are you sure it was a heart attack?" the man asked Chief Daily.

"You're the dang coroner," Chief Daily snapped as two police officers walked out of the lobby with Hawk. Chief Daily motioned for them to drive back into town. "You two get back in town. Detective Hawk will take over from here. And you," he said, pointing at the coroner, "I want an autopsy performed by tonight."

"I was going to take Alice out to dinner tonight," the coroner objected, slapping at a bug. Nikki shook her head. The coroner was dressed like he'd never left the seventies.

"By tonight," Chief Daily grumbled as he walked to his car, got in, and drove away like a mad hornet.

Nikki watched the coroner scratch the back of his head and walk back into the lobby. When the coast was clear, Hawk walked to the white BMW and then waved his hand at Nikki, obviously knowing she was watching him instead of hanging out at the lake like he'd asked her to. Nikki smiled and ran to him. "The license plate is from Georgia, of all places," Nikki told Hawk.

Hawk bit the inside of his lip. "The tourist found dead is a man named Jack Johnson, age sixty-five," Hawk said, pulling a driver's license from his front pocket and handing it to Nikki. "He's from Atlanta."

Nikki studied the driver's license. Wishing she had her reading glasses, she squinted down at the print. "Doesn't ring a bell," she said and then focused on the address posted on the license. "Hey, I know where this address—well, the area is a real posh part of Atlanta."

"He was staying on the lower floor in room two, the Deep Woods room. Each room has a theme," Hawk said, a little embarrassed.

Nikki nodded her head. "I love theme rooms," she said, focusing on the face on the driver's license. But then she suddenly looked up at Hawk. "Every room has a theme?" she asked.

"Yeah, why?" Hawk asked.

"Mr. Johnson was here by himself, I presume? I don't see anyone standing around crying. Plus, his car seats only two."

"Yeah, he checked in alone," Hawk told Nikki, wishing he were down at the lake doing some fishing.

"Theme rooms," Nikki said, feeling her gut tug at her. "Hawk, when did Mr. Johnson check in?"

"Last night, late...about 12:40 am," Hawk explained. "He didn't have a reservation, if that's what you're getting at."

"Are there any other guests staying here?" Nikki asked, looking around at the vacant parking spaces.

"The lodge is reserved for a ladies' club that's coming in a few days from now, so Mr. and Mrs. Snowfield have stopped renting rooms. They do all the cleaning themselves, from what they told me, and they didn't want the rooms they have ready to be messed up."

"Then why did they rent a room to Mr. Johnson?" Nikki asked.

Hawk shrugged. "Mr. Snowfield said the man looked like he needed to rest."

"I wonder if Mr. Johnson was traveling toward Canada or coming back?" Nikki asked Hawk, handing him back the driver's license. "You said the border is three miles north of here. If he didn't have a reservation, it's obvious he was coming back or heading toward the border."

Hawk stuffed the driver's license back down into his pants pocket. "Come on," he told Nikki, walking to the Deep Woods room. "The body is still inside, so don't get sick on me, okay?"

"I'll...be okay," Nikki promised in a quick but uncertain voice.

2

Hawk studied Nikki's face and then pushed open a thick, wooden door. The smell of fresh pine shot out of the room and struck Nikki in the face. Taking a deep breath, she followed Hawk in. Not knowing exactly what to expect, Nikki was amazed when she walked into a large room lined with a thick brown carpet that, to her delight, was very cozy. The walls were painted with murals that represented thick, deep wilderness covered in snow. On the far back wall was a stone fireplace. Two rocking chairs sat in front of the fireplace, close to a king-sized bed. A brown couch sat in the corner next to a tan reading chair. In front of the couch and chair was a wooden coffee table. A small breakfast bar stood on the left wall, holding a microwave and mini-fridge. At the back of the room, Nikki saw a door that led into a comfortable-sized bathroom. But Nikki's delight in the room quickly dissipated when she saw the dead man lying on the bed.

Hawk walked over to the body and bent over to examine it. "Nice suit...nails well-kept...mustache trimmed nicely...hair neatly cut...no signs of a struggle."

Bravely, to prove to Hawk that she wasn't squeamish, Nikki eased over to the bed. A man wearing a nice blue suit lay there. For all intents and purposes, the man looked very peaceful, as if he were simply sleeping and having a pleasant dream. "Hawk, I heard the coroner ask Chief Daily if this man died of a heart attack."

Hawk glanced at Nikki. "Does a man die of a heart attack lying in this position?" he asked. "He's lying on top of the bed covers, too. But look around the edges, the edges are smoothed. He was placed down onto the bed."

"I was about to tell you the same thing," Nikki said, lowering her eyes down onto the body. "His arms are crossed over his chest. And look around this room, not a single item out of place. The phone is still on the hook. And," Nikki said, pointing at a gray suitcase sitting next to the breakfast bar, "the suitcase isn't even opened."

"Pop insists this is a clear case of a man dying of a heart attack," Hawk told Nikki.

Nikki refocused her attention on the dead man's face. "His face is a little blue. How long has he been dead, do you think?

"Coroner examined the body earlier if that's what you can call that guy. He claims the body has been dead for a while—maybe ten hours. It's almost lunchtime, so that puts his death somewhere after 1:00 am and before 3:00 am."

"You need to ask Mr. and Mrs. Snowfield how Mr. Johnson looked when he arrived," Nikki told Hawk.

"Good idea," Hawk agreed. "I'll run this guy through the system and see what I can come up with. Right now, all we can do is wait for the autopsy report." Hawk walked away from the bed and went to the suitcase. Nikki followed. "Let's see what we have."

Nikki watched Hawk lift the suitcase up onto the breakfast bar and open it. "No clothes," she said, shocked.

"Empty," Hawk said and then began to feel around the inside of the suitcase, hoping to find a hidden compartment. Coming up empty-handed, he closed it. "Now why would a man carry an empty suitcase into a room?"

Nikki looked at Hawk. "To fill the suitcase with money."

"Bingo," Hawk agreed, nodding his head.

"Drug deal maybe?" Nikki suggested.

"I don't know. Each room is assigned a key instead of those plastic key cards. There wasn't any sign of forced entry, and the Snowfields didn't report seeing any strange vehicles on the property." Motioning toward the bathroom, he walked to it. He opened the bathroom door, reached his hand into the darkness, flipped on a light, and stepped inside. Nikki followed. "Clean as a whistle."

Nikki studied the bathroom's hardwood floor and wooden walls. It was indeed spotless. She watched Hawk examine the bathroom. "Mr. Johnson wasn't planning on staying the night," she told Hawk.

"That's my guess, too," he said. Walking Nikki out of the bathroom, he checked around the bedroom again and then went outside. "Okay," he said, "get behind the trees. After the body is carried away, we'll head back into town."

Nikki jogged to the trees. Patiently, she watched Hawk summon the coroner. The coroner hurried to his car and pulled out a black stretcher holding a body bag. Asking for Hawk's assistance, he pushed the stretcher to Mr. Johnson's room. Hawk opened the door to the room and moved aside. As the coroner pushed the stretcher through the door, Nikki saw a young man exit the front lobby, look around, and then walk back inside. "Curious," she whispered.

Thirty minutes later, Nikki was sitting in the jeep heading back toward town. "Who was the young man I saw?" she asked Hawk, watching beautiful countryside pass by.

"The grandson," Hawk explained. "Zach Snowfield, age twenty-four."

"Why didn't you tell me about him?"

"Because I knew you would immediately suspect him of killing Mr. Johnson," Hawk answered frankly. "Nikki, the kid has a mental disorder, he can barely talk. He came to stay with his grandparents because his own parents got tired of dealing with him."

Nikki grew silent. In her mind she saw a young, handsome face covered with stringy blond hair. The face she saw was intelligent if not brilliant. "Maybe," she said, uncertainly. "Drop me off back at my cabin, okay?"

"I was thinking maybe we could grab some lunch."

"Later," Nikki smiled and patted Hawk's arm. "I really need to get to my store and see how Lidia and Tori are doing."

Hawk understood. "You got it," he promised Nikki. "But do me a favor, stay away from the lodge, okay? Don't go snooping around out there. The body is gone, you saw the room, the suitcase is in the back of my jeep, the BMW is being hauled into the station, so keep away, okay?"

Nikki hid her right hand and crossed her fingers. "I don't think I'll be going back to the lodge anymore today," she said. *But tomorrow I will*, she thought.

"Good. And remember, not a word about this case to anyone," Hawk told Nikki, wondering if his new partner was telling him the truth.

3

After dropping Nikki off at her cabin, Hawk waved goodbye. Nikki waved back, and then, waiting until he was out of sight, she ran to her SUV, jumped in, and zoomed into town. She rushed into her store, politely maneuvered between chocolate-hungry tourists, and made her way into the back office. Lidia told Tori to watch the store and followed Nikki.

"Where have you been?" Lidia asked, watching Nikki set her purse down on the desk.

"I was with Hawk," Nikki said, sitting down.

"Oh," Lidia grinned, wiping some flour off of the green blouse she was wearing.

Nikki sighed. "I'm not ready for a relationship," she reminded Lidia. "Call Tori back here, okay?"

"Not until you tell me what's going on," Lidia demanded. Reading Nikki's face, she knew her boss was dealing with something secretive. Plopping down on the corner of the desk, she glared down at Nikki.

"Lidia," Nikki asked, easing her eyes toward the open office door, "what do you know about the Elk Horn Lodge?"

"Oh," Lidia said, thinking and following Nikki's eyes to the open office door, "not much. Herbert and I have never stayed there, if that's what you want to know. I wish I could be more help, but we only pass by the lodge when we drive up that way to take day-trips into Canada."

Disappointed that Lidia couldn't provide more detailed information about the lodge, Nikki tried to think. Even though she was planning to send Tori out to the lodge, she began to wonder if having Lidia accompany her might not be a bad idea. "What about Tori, would she know about the lodge?"

Lidia shook her head. "I wouldn't think so. Besides, Tori isn't from here. She moved here when she was sixteen to live with her aunt."

Nikki noticed Lidia say 'aunt' as if the word were poison in her mouth. Making a quick decision, she nodded her head. "Okay," she said and motioned for Lidia to lean down, "here's what's going on. A man has been found dead in his room at the lodge and—"

"Oh my!" Lidia gasped.

"This information cannot leave this office," Nikki warned. "This man is from Georgia...Atlanta, to be exact. I'm sure this fact is not sitting well with Chief Daily. I'm expecting a visit here at any time. That's why I rushed to the store. I was at the lodge with Hawk earlier. He's allowing me to help him on this case."

"Honey," Lidia begged, "wasn't your last adventure

enough? You helped bring down a corrupt mayor and expose the German mafia while solving the murder of a man who was lower than a skunk."

"You make it sound like I made national headlines," Nikki told Lidia. "A small-town mayor was arrested, and a few criminals hiding in town were exposed for what they were, so what? That's small change, Lidia."

"You did solve a man's murder," Lidia pointed out.

"The mayor solved the murder by confessing to the woman he went to kill," Nikki corrected Lidia.

"You're not going to take any credit, are you?"

"I was...a little green," Nikki confessed. "I did get my feet wet, though, and that felt nice."

"So let your feet dry off," Lidia begged. "Honey, let Hawk do his job. You have a nice store that's doing very well. A lot of the locals have been in wanting to see you, too. You're a big hit. Your place as a permanent resident here is sealed."

"A man from Atlanta, Georgia has been found dead," Nikki emphasized to Lidia. "If this gets out, people are going to look directly at me, and Hawk knows that. He's being calm, but he knows that soon I'm going to be the number one suspect. On the last case, I acted in order to protect myself before I learned all the facts. Lidia, I have to protect myself on this case, too."

"I have to admit, it is a little strange, since you moved here from that area," Lidia told Nikki. "If I didn't know you the way I did, I openly admit that I would suspect you, dear."

"Exactly," Nikki pointed out. "Lidia, I need you and Tori

to go out to the lodge, pretend you want a room, and look around. I can't take a chance getting caught out there. If I'm seen at the lodge, then I'll be tagged for sure."

Lidia stared at Nikki for a long time and then stood up. Quickly closing the office door, she looked at her employer as if she were insane. "Honey, a man has been found dead, and you're asking Tori and me to place ourselves in harm's way?"

"Kinda," Nikki admitted nervously. "Lidia, I need you and Tori to go to the lodge and pretend to be tourists on your way to Canada. Let me explain why." Lidia listened as Nikki described the young man she had seen at the lodge. "I need for Tori to be a little...well, flirtatious."

"Assuming that young man even comes to the front counter," Lidia pointed out.

"Yes," Nikki agreed in a heavy voice. "There is no guarantee he'll even be around. But if he is, I need for you two to see if he acts mentally ill the way Hawk described."

"And you think this young man is the killer?"

"I'm not sure," Nikki confessed. "One step at a time, okay? I'll watch the store...and I'll throw in a bonus!" she added, hoping to bribe Lidia into agreeing.

Hearing a knock at the office door, Lidia turned and opened it. Tori peeped her head in. Again, Nikki couldn't get over how beautiful the young woman was. But as always, Tori was wearing a small t-shirt over a pair of jeans and looking defeated and sad. "It's kinda busy out here; I need some help," she told Nikki in an apologetic voice.

"Of course, dear." Lidia smiled and hurried out into the store.

Tori turned to follow, but Nikki called her into the office. "Yes, Ms. Bates?" Tori asked nervously.

"Tori, honey..." Nikki began to speak, wondering how she was going to convince the young woman to risk the halls of homicide, "can you keep a secret?"

"A secret?" Tori asked. "I...yes, I can keep a secret."

Diving into dangerous waters, Nikki explained to Tori about the man found dead at Elk Horn Lodge, and then, diving into deeper waters, she explained to Tori the favor she needed. "I know I'm asking a lot, but I don't see any real danger in this. I'm sure you and Lidia will be fine."

"A man from Atlanta," Tori whispered, "Nikki, that's where you're from."

"I'm actually from a town north of Atlanta, but yes, I lived in Atlanta before moving to Vermont," Nikki admitted.

"My goodness, everyone will think you're involved somehow. I mean, your name is all over town. There's some people who are upset that you had the mayor arrested. They're claiming he had a nervous breakdown and didn't deserve to go to jail. Other people are happy about what you did...well, most people, as a matter of fact," Tori explained, keeping her eyes on the ground.

Gently, Nikki stood up, walked to Tori, and lifted her chin with her finger. "Dear, don't be shy or afraid to look me in the eyes. I'm your friend. I care about you."

Tori blushed and quickly looked down. "I know," she said in a shaky voice.

Unable to help herself, Nikki reached out and hugged the young woman. "Oh, I wish you were my own daughter," she said. "Let's just forget my idea of sending you and Lidia out to the lodge, okay?"

Shocked that Nikki was hugging her, Tori felt something inside her heart move. Closing her eyes, she drew in a deep breath and hugged Nikki back. "I'll go to the lodge," she announced. "We have to help you."

"Are you sure?" Nikki asked, letting go of Tori and looking her in the eyes.

Tori nodded her head. "Ms. Bates, you have been very kind to me. I...really like you. Please, let me help you."

"Such a brave girl," Nikki said and hugged Tori again. "Okay, here's what I need you to do. This young man might actually be mentally ill, or he might be simply pretending to be mentally ill. All I need for you to do, if he's there, is to flirt with him some. Don't throw an entire bottle of perfume at him, but spray some in the air and see how he reacts."

"I'll do my best," Tori promised.

"I'll wait here at the store," Nikki said and walked Tori out of the office.

Lidia was helping a customer. When she saw Tori's face, she sighed miserably. After helping the customer and ringing up a sale, she walked to Tori, took her hand, and told Nikki they would be back before closing time. Nikki watched Lidia and Tori leave, said a quick prayer for their safety, and then began attending to the customers in her store. It wasn't long before she got caught up in the motions of dealing with customers, handing out samples, bagging chocolates, and ringing up sales. For a few hours she completely forgot that earlier in the morning she had seen a dead body.

4

Lidia eased her car up to the front lobby of the lodge. Scared, tense, and worried that she was placing Tori's life in danger, she turned off the ignition. Taking in a deep breath of the strawberry car scent hanging on the rear-view mirror, she studied the front lobby. "We're just checking the prices," she explained. "We get in there and then get out."

Tori let her eyes walk around. The lodge was beautiful. Every fiber in her being wanted to rush to the lake and go swimming. "It's so beautiful," she said.

"Beauty can be deceiving," Lidia warned Tori. "Okay, we can't sit all day. Let's go, but if anything happens, you run, do you understand me? I won't let anything happen to you. I've grown very fond of you, Tori."

Tori looked at Lidia. She had no idea that the woman cared for her so deeply. "We'll be okay," she promised.

Getting out of the car, Tori walked with Lidia up to the

lobby entrance. Giving Tori a 'use-caution' eye, she pulled open a wooden door and stepped through. Tori followed. Together they entered a cozy front room that had a magnificent stone fireplace. Walking across a soft brown carpet hugging log walls, Lidia and Tori both were captivated by the appealing atmosphere and rustic design. "Beautiful," Lidia whispered.

"It sure is," Tori agreed, taking it all in. The smell of pine was thick in the air, mingled with the scent of fireplace smoke from the previous winter.

Lidia quickly nudged Tori with her elbow and nodded at a wooden front counter. The young man Nikki had seen step outside the lobby earlier stood up from a black office chair. "Help you?" he asked in a voice that seemed far too impolite, Lidia noticed.

"Yes, my niece and I are going to vacation in this area for a week, and we're checking prices," Lidia said, approaching the counter and drawing the young man's features into her memory. The face staring across the front counter at her did not appear to be the face of someone who was mentally ill...or did it?

Tori quickly jumped into character. Offering a cute smile, she forced her eyes to make contact. "It's very nice here. I love the lake."

"Yeah, the lake is nice," the young man told Tori, taking in her beauty the way a wolf looks at an innocent rabbit. "Listen, ladies, we're expecting a large group in a few days. We don't have any vacancies. Try someplace in town, okay?"

"Oh, but the lake, Aunt Milda," Tori pouted, throwing a

Peppermint Chocolate Murder

fake name into the air.

"Well, I'm sure we'll find a nice hotel to stay at. This one does seem a little out of our budget," Lidia told Tori. "We're sorry to have bothered you."

"No bother," the young man said and smiled at Tori. "Maybe we'll see each other around?"

"Maybe," Tori smiled back. Walking back outside with Lidia, she quickly got in the car. Lidia, not wanting to seem suspicious, eased away from the lodge and raced back toward town. "What a jerk," Tori said in a disgusted voice.

"He's not mentally ill," Lidia pointed out, "not in the sense Hawk wants Nikki to believe."

Tori sunk down into her seat. "Ms. Bates is in real trouble, isn't she?"

Regretfully, Lidia nodded her head yes. Easing her foot off the gas pedal, she slowed down to the prescribed speed limit. Looking out at the beautiful landscape, she knew that once word got around about the death of a man from Georgia, Nikki Bates would be in some serious hot water. "That woman has a dark cloud following her."

"She's so nice," Tori told Lidia. "She...hugged me. I haven't been hugged in a very long time."

"That woman would adopt you if she could," Lidia pointed out. "The question is, what do we do now? Tori, honey, I'm getting to be an old lady. I can't become involved in dangerous things like this. I have Herbert to think about. I have our future to think about and...I'm sitting here making up a bunch of miserable excuses as to why I shouldn't help a friend."

"We'll help Ms. Bates," Tori promised Lidia.

Lidia didn't speak again until she and Tori were safely back in the store. When they walked in, they found Chief Daily talking to Nikki. "Just come down to the station when you close up," he told Nikki, and he walked out of the store, indifferent to the customers and how his presence might affect them.

"You handle the customers," Lidia told Tori and pulled Nikki into the office. "What did he want?"

Nikki closed the office door. "He wants to question me," Nikki told Lidia, shaking her head. "You're back earlier than I thought you would be."

"Your mystery boy was sitting behind the front counter," Lidia explained. "Nikki, honey, that boy isn't at all the way Hawk describes him to be. In fact, he's very handsome and, as you said, appears to be very smart. Except for acting like a wolf toward Tori, he was a cold fish, too."

"So he's pretending to be mentally ill, but if he was sitting at the front counter..." Nikki began to think as she paced around the cramped office. "Mr. and Mrs. Snowfield may be hiding his little act..."

"I didn't see them," Lidia told Nikki sitting down at the desk. "The boy did mention something about a ladies' group that was due to arrive in a few days."

"He did?" Nikki asked. "That's very interesting. I might have to take a look at that guest list. I'll ask Hawk to get the list for me."

Lidia gave Nikki a concerned face. "Chief Daily

appeared very sour when he walked out of here, honey. The man may be a nit-wit, but he is still Chief of Police, and that position comes with certain powers."

Nikki returned Lidia's concerned looks with knowing eyes. "I have Hawk on my side, and he'll help me balance the scales some. That's what friends are for, right?"

"We both know Hawk wants to be more than just friends with you," Lidia pointed out. "You could do worse, dear. Hawk is a good man."

"I'm not ready," Nikki reiterated. "Lidia, I loved my ex-husband. I explained to you how we met. It was love at first sight. At times I want to call him just to hear his voice, and at other times I want to strangle him. I know our marriage has dissolved, and I'm...accepting that truth. Even if I were still married, I wouldn't be happy. My ex-husband has moved on with his life, and so have I, but old wounds take time to heal. My heart isn't ready to open up to the notion of allowing someone else into my life. I agree that Hawk is a nice man, but if he cares about me, he'll be my friend."

"Give it time," Lidia said and offered Nikki a loving, motherly smile. "So," she said, taking a deep breath, "I guess I better get back into the ball game and go help Tori with some of our customers."

"Thanks," Nikki said and quickly hugged Lidia. "I'm going to go home and grab a bite to eat before I go see Chief Daily."

Lidia didn't believe Nikki. "Where are you really going?" she asked, concerned.

"Honestly, I'm going home," Nikki promised. "I need some time to think matters over. If I know Hawk, he'll be at the police station when I arrive. I'm guessing he's going to ask me to eat dinner with him...as friends. At least I hope he does. I need to find out what he's come up with so far."

5

After leaving her store, Nikki eased through town as quietly as possible, admiring the relaxed tourists roaming from shop to shop, standing outside on the sidewalks, holding small dogs on tight leashes, sipping cold drinks, talking, laughing, and enjoying life. Even though Nikki knew there wasn't a person in the world who didn't have a problem or two, the tourists she passed seemed to be without a single care or concern. Thinking back to the trips she had taken with her husband when they were first married, Nikki remembered walking around cozy little towns the same way the tourists in her town were doing...just walking hand-in-hand with her husband, forgetting all her cares, melting into the moment.

Feeling tears begin to well up in her eyes, Nikki pushed her old memories away and packed them back in a tight trunk where they belonged. "Let's focus on the case at hand," she told herself as she drove out of town.

Back at her cabin, Nikki sat down at the kitchen table with a cup of hot cocoa. Sure, it was hot outside, but cocoa always lifted her sad mood. Taking careful sips, she savored the creamy taste of the cocoa mixed in with a little milk. Closing her eyes, she stretched her ears to hear the sounds of the soft jazz playing on her computer in the living room. "Okay," she whispered, "let's think. A man from your part of the country was found dead in a room three miles from the Canadian border with an empty suitcase. The man lived in a posh part of Atlanta, drove a very nice BMW, and dressed to impress. But all that is a farce, isn't it?"

Nikki walked her mind back to the lodge, wandered up to the parked BMW, studied the car for a few minutes, and then crept inside the Deep Woods room. Walking up to the bed, she cast her eyes down onto the face of Mr. Johnson. "What were you doing here?" she asked, examining the man's peaceful slumber. "You were here to accept money or drugs, and then drive into Canada, but how would you have crossed the border?"

Nikki bit down on her lower lip. "I need to see the border," she said.

Forcing her body to remain seated, Nikki calmly sipped her hot cocoa. Not having seen the Canadian border that sat north of her new town, she wasn't sure what to expect. The road leading up to the border was a simple two-lane back road that exhausted snow plows during the winter season. "If I was in a hurry to cross into Canada as quietly as possible, I would take a back road, too," Nikki said, finally standing up. Walking to the kitchen sink, she rinsed out the cup, hurried to the bathroom, and then made tracks toward the front door. Right before she could open the front door, someone knocked.

Startled, Nikki stepped back. Feeling her heart racing, she carefully called out, "Who is it?"

"Hawk."

Relieved, Nikki opened the front door, but to her disappointment, Chief Daily was also standing on the front porch. "Out here," he told Nikki in an impatient voice.

Nikki looked at Hawk. Hawk gave her a 'this is important' look. Closing the front door behind her with her purse in hand, Nikki stepped out onto the front porch. "You didn't have to come to my home. I told you I would make a trip to the station at the set time," she told Chief Daily in an annoyed voice, hoping that her demeanor hid her worry.

"Ms. Bates, my son ran Mr. Johnson through the system," Chief Daily said in a rough voice. "It seems that this Mr. Johnson is a ghost. We can't even get anything off the man's prints, for crying out loud."

"Not a thing," Hawk told Nikki, supporting Chief Daily's statement. "The driver's license has to be a fake. The BMW was stolen. Seems we have a shadow on our hands."

"What about the address on the driver's license?" Nikki asked and then realized she had said too much.

"What?" Chief Daily asked, gritting his teeth. "How do you..." Looking at Hawk with angry eyes, he shook his head. "I should have known."

"The address belongs to a house that burnt down eight days ago," Hawk told Nikki, ignoring Chief Daily's anger.

"Nikki, I can't even get a facial recognition match on this guy in the system. Whoever this guy is, he's a John Doe right now."

"Where were you last night?" Chief Daily fired at Nikki. "I want answers, do you hear me?"

"Not in that tone of voice," Nikki fired back. Having dealt with her share of angry policemen in the past, she wasn't about to back down from Chief Daily, even though she was worried about her own situation. "You can speak to me with the proper amount of respect or leave my property at once. This is America, and I still have my rights under the Constitution. So unless you're placing me under arrest, you can shove it in your eye, Chief."

Hawk grinned and then wiped at his lip with his finger. Glancing at Chief Daily, he watched the man's face turn red as a firecracker. But what could he do? Nikki was right. Hawk knew that his pop was walking on thin ice, and if he wasn't careful, he was liable to have a harassment case thrown at him. "Ms. Bates," Chief Daily said, lowering his tone while taking deep breaths, "where were you last night between midnight and three o'clock?"

"Here, making chocolate," Nikki answered Chief Daily in a calm tone. "I made peppermint chocolate fudge until...oh, two o'clock, and then I went to bed. I slept until eight. Hawk arrived at nine for morning coffee."

"You two are real cozy," Chief Daily told Hawk. Throwing his eyes out onto the lovely front lawn, he shook his head. "That lodge needs security cameras," he complained. "All right, Ms. Bates, you're in the clear for now, but stay in town."

"Where else would I go?" Nikki asked in a voice that told Chief Daily his statement was absurd.

Chief Daily squeezed his hands together. "Listen," he snapped, forgetting his patience, "you're bad luck for this town, do you hear me? Ever since you arrived, nothing but bad things have occurred. I just so happen to think our mayor didn't deserve you destroying his life. The man was being blackmailed—"

"The man was a criminal who attempted to murder an innocent woman," Nikki yelled, feeling her own patience leave the tracks. "There is a system of law in this country, Chief, and no one is above the law. This town is safer now, and I, for one, am glad."

"You made a few enemies," Chief Daily warned Nikki, "so I wouldn't be going around town parading your victory."

"She also made a lot of friends," Hawk pointed out. "Sure, some people are sour, but more people are grateful to Nikki. Every town has bad grapes, Pop, and you know that. Who cares if a few old bats are upset with Nikki for making this town a better place for our children. And if you had done your job, maybe you would have realized that the mayor was hiding members of the mafia here, for crying out loud."

"Don't lecture me!" Chief Daily hollered at Hawk. "We're already on thin ice here."

"Don't remind me," Hawk growled back, allowing Nikki to see his temper. But, Nikki realized, the temper she saw erupt in Hawk's eyes was a controlled temper, the kind of temper a brilliant man utilized with patience and skill instead of with uncontrolled arrogance. "This town was polluted long before Nikki moved here."

"That's not what people are going to think once word of this man's death gets out," Chief Daily pointed out. "People are going to put two and two together. Even the people who support this woman will lose confidence in her."

"So be it," Nikki said, stepping up to Hawk and standing at his side. "I'm not leaving town. I can clearly see that's what you want me to do. I'm staying right here."

"There's ways to make a person leave town," Chief Daily promised Nikki.

"Did you just threaten me?" Nikki asked, shocked.

Chief Daily began to defend his actions and then realized that, yes, he had come right out in the open and threatened an innocent woman. What in the world was wrong with him? He had just crossed a red line without any cause or justification to do so other than he disliked Nikki on a personal level. "I'm sorry, I didn't mean..."

Shocked and hurt that the Chief of Police would resort to threats, Nikki dashed away to her SUV. "Jerk," Hawk snapped at Chief Daily and brushed past him with a hard shoulder.

"I didn't mean..." Chief Daily tried again to explain and then fell silent. Ashamed of his actions, he watched Hawk reach Nikki just as the woman began backing down the driveway. Ignoring Hawk, Nikki backed onto the grass to avoid Hawk's jeep, eased out onto the road, and pulled away.

"Nikki!" Hawk yelled, throwing his arms up into the air. Looking back at Chief Daily he shook his head. "What's wrong with you? Why did you threaten her?" he yelled. "We both know she didn't have anything to do with that man's death."

With tears in her eyes, Nikki set a route toward the Canadian border. "Maybe I will leave town," she whispered to herself. "Maybe I'm not meant to be here after all. I can always go back to Atlanta and get my old job."

6

Without any real reasoning behind her actions, Nikki stopped at the lodge before driving farther north to the Canadian border. Sure, she was taking a risky chance, but so what? Who at the lodge knew her? The local paper had printed her name in the story about the mayor, but her face had not been posted. Even if the owners of the lodge had read the story about her —which they probably did—they didn't know her face unless they'd paid a visit to her store, which, Nikki thought as she parked in front of the lobby, wasn't likely. Besides, if her gut was right, the Snowfields weren't the type of people to make casual visits into town. The lodge required a great deal of work, maintenance, and management, which they handled all on their own.

Examining the front lobby, Nikki drew in a deep breath. The land, the lobby, and the air were clean, fresh and beautiful. The thought of sitting in standstill traffic in Atlanta almost caused an ulcer to form in her stomach.

Gripping her purse, she walked up to the front door of the lobby, pulled it open, stepped inside, and was immediately struck by a strange and wonderful rustic beauty. "Help you?" a cold voice asked.

Putting a friendly smile on her face, Nikki walked up to the front counter. "I want a room, please," she told the young man, who didn't appear mentally ill at all.

"We're not renting out rooms right now. Rooms are all booked because a group is arriving in a few days," the young man told Nikki.

Nikki scanned the young man's gray t-shirt and then looked back up to his face. She lost her smile. It was time to get down to the nitty-gritty. "Fine, I'm not here for a room. I'm here, Zach, to find out about you."

"How do you know my name?" Zach asked Nikki, narrowing his eyes and forcing his face to become cold and angry.

"I thought you could barely speak?" she asked. "You seem to be speaking very clearly now. Detective Hawk might be interested in knowing you pulled the wool over his eyes. Maybe I will give him a call."

Zach stared at Nikki with hard eyes. "Who are you?" he demanded.

"Who are you?" Nikki asked back, "and why are you pretending to be mentally ill in the eyes of the police? Earlier two women came in here and you didn't act shy in front of them."

Zach thought back to Tori. Folding his arms, he tried to think. "I hate cops, okay? I've had my share of trouble with them in the past. My folks ditched me with my grandparents because they got tired of dealing with me. It's not much different here; earlier today a man was found dead in his room. What do my grandparents do? They tell me to act stupid because they don't want the police thinking I had anything to do with it. So I did what they asked me...maybe a little too good."

"Where are your grandparents now?" Nikki demanded.

"The old woman is upstairs, and the old man is down by the lake doing something," Zach explained. "Want me to go and get her?"

"Why are you watching the front desk?" Nikki asked instead. "Are you waiting for someone, Zach?"

Zach tensed. "What are you, a modern day Nancy Drew or something? The old woman ordered me to watch the lobby, okay? I'm told, and I quote, that I will 'earn my right to live here' by pulling my own weight," Zach finished in a disgusted voice.

Nikki focused on Zach's eyes. The young man standing before her was bitter, angry, and a real pain to society, but he wasn't lying to her. And, Nikki concluded, he wasn't a killer, either. Sarcastic, yes. Disrespectful, yes. Bitter, yes...a killer, no. "I can run you through the system, but you can save us both a lot of time by telling me what you have on your record."

Zach shrugged his shoulders. "Few fights, got caught spray-painting a police car, broke a few windows, went for a few joy rides...nothing major."

"Maybe not to you," Nikki pointed out.

"Hey, lady, I was just having some fun," Zach told

Nikki, unfolding his arms. "Take a hike. I'm done talking to you."

"A man was found dead," Nikki yanked Zach back into the conversation, "and that is very, very serious."

"I didn't kill the guy," Zach told Nikki, staring at her with angry eyes, "I found the body, but I didn't kill him."

"You found the body?" Nikki asked.

Zach kicked himself for spilling the beans. "Yeah...yeah, I found the body, okay? I know my grandparents told the police they did, but they lied. So go ahead and arrest us."

"Zach, what time did you find the body? Listen to me, I'm not a cop. I'm a private detective. I'm not interested in arresting anyone. I only want the truth," Nikki confessed.

Zach grinned. "A female detective...say, you're kind of a babe, too and—"

Nikki leaned across the counter and slapped Zach across his face. "I'm not a babe. You will show respect, or next time I'll knock you cold."

Zach stumbled backward. No one had ever slapped him in the face before. Startled and shocked, he stared at Nikki's angry face. And then he simply felt ashamed of his actions. Maybe acting like a jerk all the time wasn't the key. "I found the body around nine," he told Nikki, rubbing his cheek. "The guy asked for a wake-up call at that time. When he didn't pick up the phone in his room, I went and knocked on his door."

"Keep going."

"The door to the room wasn't locked. It was open, but barely. I didn't care. I knocked on the door and then pushed it open," Zach explained. "I didn't tell the cops this. They think the old man found the guy dead after taking towels to the room."

"You open the door and walk in, then what?" Nikki asked.

"I see the guy lying on the bed, so I tell him who I am," Zach explained. "The guy didn't answer, so I walked over to the bed and shook his leg, thinking he was passed out or something...long story short, the guy was dead. I didn't hang around. I ran and got the old man."

Nikki considered Zach's story. There was something Zach was hiding from her, something very important. "What about the suitcase?"

Nikki saw Zach tense up again. "Hey, I didn't touch anything in that guy's room," he said in a defensive tone. "I got the old man and didn't step foot back in the room."

Nikki took her eyes away from Zach and studied the front lobby. "Okay, Zach, thank you for the information. I'm leaving now. You can tell the cops I came by, and your grandparents as well if you—"

"Listen, lady," Zach said, watching his tone, "my grandparents couldn't care less about me, okay? I'm here because it was either them or jail. I'm not their answering service. If you want to come by later and talk with them, that's your business. And as far as the cops go, they can go stand in traffic."

"Okay," Nikki told Zach as she walked to the lobby door. Pausing, she turned and faced him. "I knew a kid once who had great potential but also had a huge chip on his shoulder. He ended up going to prison for robbing a bank because he got caught up with the wrong people."

"So?" Zach asked.

"Let me finish," Nikki told Zach. "While he was in prison, he was stabbed in the back. My friend almost died. It took him a while to realize that the world wasn't against him and that every bad choice he made was his own fault. So he stopped blaming other people and got his life back on track. After getting out of prison he went back to school, and then college, and today he's a school teacher."

"Aw, gee, how nice," Zach replied. Shaking his head, he looked down at his feet. "Hey, lady, I'm sorry, I get what you mean. I know I made some bad choices, I get that, but people just won't stop riding my back all the time. I'm just a failure in their eyes, someone to tolerate because I'm family."

"Can I ask you a question?"

"Yeah, what is it?" Zach looked at Nikki.

"What do you want to do with your life?"

Zach shrugged his shoulders. "I'm pretty good at fixing cars, you know. My old man is a mechanic. I'm not too bad with a hammer and nail, either."

"Great," Nikki said, "you have skills then. But Zach, what you do with your skills is up to you. Honey, this world will chew you up alive and spit you out. I know it's hard, and I know that sometimes the choices we make can harm our future. But you can overcome them if you want— the choice is yours. But remember, before you can earn respect from other people, you have to respect yourself first. Okay?"

"A nobody like me?" Zach asked. "I'm supposed to respect a loser?"

"You're not a loser," Nikki promised Zach. "I need to go, but we'll see each other again. I...Zach, I know you're hiding something, and in time I hope you tell me what you're hiding. But I'm not going to force you. When you begin to respect yourself and want to change, you will tell me what you're hiding. Goodbye."

Nikki left Zach feeling like a deer caught in a pair of headlights. In all truth, she realized, Zach wasn't a horrible person, not as horrible as she had first thought. Misguided, angry, upset, hurt, confused...yes, but definitely not a killer. Walking to her SUV, she paused. In the distance, she saw an old man walking up toward the lodge with a shovel in his hand. The old man was too far away to recognize Nikki. Quickly, Nikki jumped into her SUV and pulled away, hoping to appear inconspicuous.

"Next stop, the Canadian border," she said, pulling onto the two-lane back road and driving north. Driving past beautiful landscape, she thought about Zach and the suitcase. "If there was money in the suitcase..." Nikki struggled to put the case together in her mind.

7

Nikki eased to a stop in front of a run-down wooden shack acting as a border station. The shack was severely waterlogged and no bigger than a closet. Nikki didn't even spot a crossing pole. Instead, as she sat waiting in her SUV, she saw a man who had to be older than time walk out of the shack and wave one hand at her to drive forward while holding a clipboard in his other hand. Nikki nodded her head and eased her SUV forward. Rolling down her driver's side window, she smiled at the old man who was wearing a wrinkled border patrol uniform. "Hi," she said in a cheerful voice.

"Driver's license," the old man said in a bored tone, "and the reason for the visit."

"Oh, I'm not going into Canada," Nikki said keeping her smile, "I'm out sightseeing and wanted to see where this road led to."

"Into Canada," the old man said, looking down at Nikki. "You can turn around."

"Oh, sure," Nikki smiled and then pretended to look around. "You must get lonely being out here by yourself. My, it's a long way from town."

"I read," the old man answered Nikki in a flat voice. "Have a nice day."

"Are you here all the time?" Nikki asked quickly.

"Each shift consists of twelve hours. I work from noon to midnight, and then I go home."

"Who works from midnight to noon?" Nikki asked. "Whoever it is, he or she must be a real night owl."

The old man gave Nikki a bored face. "My brother works from midnight to noon. We're both retired."

"Wow," Nikki said, pretending to be interested. "You guys must be something special. I mean, the only thing stopping anyone from going into Canada is you."

"Ma'am," the old man said, growing impatient, "there are so many back roads around here, anyone could sneak across the border if they wanted."

"Back roads?" Nikki asked. "I didn't spot any back roads."

"That's because you didn't look," the old man scolded Nikki. "If you know where to look, you'll find one or two of them. Now, good day to you."

Nikki watched the old man return to his shack. "Back roads," Nikki whispered, backing up and driving back toward town. Slowing down the SUV, she studied each side of the road, trying to spot any sign of a back road which was probably nothing more than an illegal dirt trail. But when she reached the lodge, Nikki gave up. Driving past the lodge, she debated whether to drive back to town or turn around. "It's getting late. I'll search again tomorrow," Nikki promised.

Driving back to her store, she saw Hawk's jeep parked out front. Shaking her head, she put on a brave face and walked inside. Lidia and Tori were closing down the store. Tori was sweeping and cleaning. Lidia was handling the paperwork. Hawk was leaning against the front counter. When he saw Nikki, he leaned up. "Where did you go?" he asked in a caring voice.

"I took a ride," Nikki replied, smiling at Tori and waving a hand at Lidia, who poked her head out of the back office. "What do you want?"

"Dinner," Hawk said, "I thought we could eat at the Jukebox, grab a burger and a milkshake and just talk. And before you say no, let me say this. I know what Pop did was wrong, and I sure gave him a chewing for it, too. He's promised to back off and let you breathe. I have some information about the case I want to go over with you. I didn't find anything on our John Doe, but I did find something on the stolen BMW."

Nikki studied Hawk's sincere face. It wasn't Hawk she was mad at, after all. And wasn't the man standing before her supposed to be her partner on the case? "Okay." Nikki offered Hawk a smile as a peace offering. "I could go for a burger and a milkshake. Tori, would you like to come? Lidia, you can go ask Herbert to meet us at the Jukebox," she called to the back office.

"I can't," Tori apologized, holding a broom in her hand. "My aunt will be expecting me."

Hawk looked at Tori and scratched the back of his head and wondered how such a pretty young lady could appear so miserable. "You're more than welcome to join us," he told Tori. "My treat."

"Oh, no really, thanks, but my aunt..." Tori apologized and hurried back to her chores.

Nikki watched Tori sweep around the shelves and front counter. "She's so sweet," she told Hawk. "Someday I'm going to have to meet this aunt of hers."

Lidia walked out of the back office with the green bank deposit bag. "Not bad," she told Nikki, handing her the deposit bag. "Everyone raved over your peppermint chocolate. We're sold out."

"I sold a lot, too, when you and Tori went...on that errand," Nikki quickly caught herself. "I'll make more tonight. I'll need to run by the grocery store and get more supplies first. Tori, honey, would you like to come over and help me make fudge tonight?"

Tori stopped sweeping. Nikki was so kind to her, and the thought of being crammed under her aunt's thumb all night saddened her. "I...well, sure, okay," she said and smiled. "I can come over if you would like. I have to cook my aunt's dinner, but after that, I will be free."

"Great," Nikki beamed, "why don't you come over around nine, and we'll cook the night away."

Lidia nudged Nikki in the side with her elbow. "Tori rides a bike to work, remember?" she whispered.

"Oh, right!" Nikki said. "Honey, I'll pick you up around nine."

Tori smiled. She really liked Nikki, and the idea of making chocolate with a woman who treated her like a daughter made her feel warm inside. "I'll be waiting."

"Will you lock up for me?" Nikki asked Lidia. "I'll go to the bank."

Lidia glanced at Hawk. "Be a gentleman," she ordered him.

Hawk threw his hands up into the air. "Hey, this isn't a date—we're just getting a few burgers. Down, tiger!"

"I'll down you with a chair over your head if you don't keep your hands where they belong," Lidia promised Hawk.

Hawk looked at Nikki and then whistled in the air. "Man, you hire some tough people, don't you? Forget the mafia, let this woman loose in the world."

"And don't you forget it," Lidia told Hawk. "Now, scoot, the both of you. Go eat. Tori and I will close up shop."

Nikki hugged Lidia. "We need to talk later. Come over to my cabin about nine," she whispered in Lidia's ear. "It's very important."

"Okay, honey," Lidia whispered back.

"Tori, I'll pick you up around nine," Nikki called out and left with Hawk.

8

Nikki was sitting in a cozy booth in a 1950s style café. An antique jukebox was shooting out a song about someone wondering about a blue moon. Relaxing, she soaked in the environment. Looking at old photos of movie stars plastered on a black-and-white checkered wall, she wondered how the world had changed so much. "Times sure have changed. Instead of Elvis, we have music that hurts my ears."

Hawk picked up a plastic menu. "I know what you mean," he agreed. "Today's music pollutes the minds of our children. Give me Elvis any day of the week."

Nikki picked up her menu. "So what about the stolen car?" she asked, feeling a few eyes staring at her from other booths.

"The BMW belonged to a Mr. Henry Greendale. Mr. Greendale owned the house that burned down. He also worked for a security firm in Atlanta," Hawk whispered over his menu. "I would speak to him, but the guy is dead."

"How?" Nikki whispered back.

"Died in the house fire," Hawk explained, keeping his voice low. "But that's not all of it. At the time of his death, Mr. Greendale was working in a major bank in Atlanta."

"When was he found dead?"

"Eight days ago," Hawk answered, "the same day his wife reported his BMW stolen."

Nikki kept her eyes on the menu. A double cheeseburger with onion rings sounded great. The rumblings in her stomach clearly told her she was past being hungry. "Money was involved then," Nikki said, lowering her menu.

Hawk nodded. "And we have an empty suitcase," he answered, putting down his own menu. "Whoever killed this guy took the money."

"Hawk," Nikki said, spotting a pretty young waitress with short black hair approaching the booth, "in a minute; here comes the waitress."

Hawk looked over and saw a young girl wearing a black and white uniform approach the booth. "Hey guys, my name is Mandy, and I'll be your waitress. What can I get you to drink?" the young woman asked, diving off into her normal waitress dialogue.

"Water with lemon for me," Nikki said.

"Coffee, black...make it decaf," Hawk ordered.

"Water with lemon and a black decaf," the waitress said and smiled. "I'll be right back."

Nikki waited until the waitress walked away and then told Hawk about visiting the old man at the border. "Pitiful...anyone could sneak in."

"I know," Hawk agreed and told Nikki that he was familiar with the poor shape of the border patrol station.

"That old man told me there were back roads. I searched, but I couldn't spot any. I'm going to search again tomorrow," Nikki explained.

Hawk looked down at his hands. "Nikki," he said, "I already checked into the back roads. There are a few. One back road..."

"What?" Nikki pressed at Hawk. "Hey, we're partners here," she said and then remembered her talk with Zach. Was she going to tell Hawk about her visit to the lodge? If not, was it really fair to press Hawk to reveal hidden information to her? Feeling guilty, she took a straw and peeled off the paper. Waiting until the waitress brought the drinks, Nikki finally looked up at Hawk, who was carefully studying her. "What?"

"You went back to the lodge, didn't you?"

"Yes," Nikki confessed.

"Nikki," Hawk said and threw his hand onto his forehead, "I told you to stay away from the lodge, didn't I?"

"Yes."

"Then why did you—wait, what am I asking? I should have known better," Hawk said, rubbing his eyes. "I might as well tell you that there is a back road that leads into Canada that is connected to the property the lodge sits on. Now before you go flying off the handle, don't assume that means—"

"That the Snowfields are somehow involved?" Nikki whispered.

"Ready to order?" the waitress asked, returning to the booth.

"I'll have the grilled chicken salad, and make it to-go, please," Nikki ordered, giving Hawk a sour look.

"Uh, I'll have...I'll stay with my coffee for now," Hawk told the waitress. When the waitress walked away, he bit the inside of his jaw and frowned. "What?"

"We're not partners anymore," Nikki answered Hawk, standing up. "I'm going to find out what is so special about the Snowfields that you're protecting them."

"I'm not protecting anyone!" Hawk said. He urged her to keep her voice low.

"Yes, you are," Nikki snapped. "I talked to Zach Snowfield, and he isn't mentally ill, Hawk. I also sent Lidia and Tori out to the lodge, and they can back up my story. You tried to push me away from that kid."

"You what? You sent who? Hawk asked, rubbing his eyes again. "Nikki, you can't do these things. I'm conducting a murder investigation here."

"Exactly," Nikki told Hawk, "you...not us," she said and walked away to the cash register.

Hawk got to his feet and followed Nikki. "You don't understand," he whispered over her shoulder.

"Leave me alone," Nikki whispered back. "And don't worry, I'm leaving town once I get this all figured out."

Hawk stopped in his tracks. Unable to say anything more, he watched Nikki pay for her salad and leave. Feeling deflated, he walked back to the booth and sat down. Putting his head down onto his hands, he closed his eyes and shook his head. "I have a choice to make," he told himself.

Upset, Nikki slowly drove around until it turned dark, thinking, trying to clear her head. After turning onto the road leading to her cabin, she saw headlights appear and come up close behind her SUV. Realizing that she was in trouble, Nikki sped up. The headlights kept pace. A few seconds later, the front end of a truck rammed the back of the SUV. Holding onto the steering wheel as tightly as possible, Nikki managed to stay on the road. Speeding up, she raced forward. The truck managed to keep pace and rammed the SUV again. With her heart racing, Nikki knew that she wasn't going to be able to outrun the truck.

Making a split-second move, Nikki sped up until the SUV was racing down the road at a dangerous speed and then slammed on her brakes. The truck smashed into the back of the SUV. The violent force of the crash activated the driver's seat airbag. Stunned and disoriented, Nikki managed to press her right foot against the brake. The truck, now damaged and with both front headlights smashed, eased back from the SUV and disappeared into the dark. Now, Nikki thought, trying to remain conscious, Hawk would be able to track the truck down when the driver tried to have it repaired. But Nikki knew who the truck belonged to.

9

After being released from the hospital, Nikki allowed Lidia to drive her home. "I'm fine," Nikki promised Lidia. "The airbag saved me from any real injury. My back is a little sore, that's all."

Lidia crept through town, past dark stores and down empty streets. "Hawk didn't believe your story," she said.

"I don't, either," Tori said from the back seat. Leaning forward, she looked at Nikki. "Ms. Bates, what really happened?"

Nikki sighed. Carefully, she explained about the truck that had attempted to run her off the road. "Now before you two panic, I don't think the driver meant to harm me. Someone wanted to scare me."

"Who?" Lidia demanded, crawling under a yellow flashing caution light hanging over the middle of Main Street.

"I can't say for sure, but I have an idea."

"Honey, I think it's time you stop involving yourself in

this case. As a matter of fact, I'm going to have to insist. You could have died tonight," Lidia said, worried.

"I can't," Nikki objected. "Not yet. I..." Nikki looked at Lidia and then to Tori. She was becoming very fond of her friends. The thought of leaving them saddened her heart. But could she really stay in town? "I won't involve you two any longer. I was wrong to do so. I'm sorry."

"Don't be sorry," Tori told Nikki and carefully touched her shoulder the way a daughter does when she tries to comfort her mother. "Ms. Bates, you have been very kind to me. I...we want to help you if you let us."

"Honey," Lidia began to object and then simply sighed. "You're not going to get off this case are you?" she asked Nikki.

"No," Nikki answered.

"Herbert isn't too happy with me being out this late," Lidia confessed. "As a matter of fact, honey, he's been pressuring me to find another job."

"And?" Nikki asked, looking at Lidia's face silhouetted in darkness.

"Herbert and I have never agreed on much. Most of the time we just agree to disagree," Lidia told Nikki. "He's a good man. It just so happens he's wrong to believe you're a bad influence."

Nikki felt her heart break. The thought of Lidia's husband condemning her behind closed doors almost brought her to tears. "I'm sorry he feels that way about me."

"A lot of people in town are happy with you," Lidia continued, "but a few are upset with you. One of the few owns the campground we live at, honey. You know Herbert and I live on a fixed income. We can't afford to rent a house...far too expensive."

"I understand," Nikki said and then rubbed her back. "Lidia, if you want to find another job, I—"

"I didn't say that," Lidia interrupted Nikki. "I went out to the lodge for you, didn't I? I don't care what people think because I see the good in you. I'm between a rock and a hard place, that's all. But what it comes down to is what my daddy once told me."

"What did your daddy tell you?" Tori asked.

"My daddy once told me that a friend—a real friend—will stand true no matter the cost," Lidia told Tori and then smiled at Nikki. "You're a jewel, honey. I'm going to stand by you, okay? I wish you would leave this case alone, but it's clear that you're not going to. So I'll do what I can to help. Herbert will just have to fuss. And if we get kicked out of the campground—"

"You can have the guest room in my cabin, permanently," Nikki told Lidia.

"Thank you, honey, but I was thinking maybe you could give your guest room to Tori."

"What?" Tori asked, shocked.

Nikki looked at Lidia. Lidia nodded her head, and Nikki understood. "That's a wonderful idea," she told Tori. "Dear, you can come and live with me, free of charge."

Tori couldn't believe her ears. But before she could say anything, a cop car pulled up behind Lidia and flashed its lights. "Oh good grief," Lidia said, pulling over to the side of the road. Rolling down the driver's side window, she waited.

Chief Daily got out of the cruiser and walked up to the driver's side window. Peering down, he looked past Lidia and straight at Nikki. "I want you to know that I have one of my men camped in your driveway. From here forth, you go nowhere without an escort."

"I..." Nikki began to speak and then stopped. What could she say? Guilt was written all over Chief Daily's face. She could clearly see the man was sorry for the remark he had made standing on her front porch earlier in the day. "Thank you, Chief Daily, that's very kind of you."

"I'm going to find that truck," Chief Daily promised Nikki and walked away.

"Well," Lidia said, rolling up the driver's side window, "our Chief of Police actually on the job. I'm impressed."

"He still wants me to leave town, I can see it in his eyes," Nikki sighed miserably. "I guess I can't blame him. His life was pretty peaceful before I showed up."

"Leave town?" Tori asked. "Ms. Bates, you're not leaving town, are you?"

"Well...I was considering it and—"

"What?" Lidia exploded.

"I...was considering it," Nikki continued in a reluctant voice, "but I really don't want to leave. I like my new home, and I'm especially fond of you two."

"If you dare try to leave we'll chain you to a tree," Lidia threatened Nikki. "Honey, I know people in this town, but that doesn't make them my friends. You're someone who I have come to care about very deeply. It...well, it feels right, the three of us girls together like this, almost as if we're a team."

"I agree," Tori said and hugged Nikki's arm. "Ms. Bates, please stay."

Nikki felt tears begin to fall from her eyes. "How can I leave?" she laughed through her tears. "Say, girls, there's an all-night diner open in my kitchen. I'm starved. Who is up for some homemade hamburgers?"

"Me," Tori raised her hand.

"As long as you make some of your famous peppermint chocolate afterward," Lidia smiled and got her car moving. "Herbert, dear, you can do your crosswords without me tonight."

10

The following morning Nikki woke up early. The night with the girls had been fun and full of laughs, and even though their night had run later than expected, her mind could not remain asleep. The one lingering question that she could not escape was: Where was Hawk? After making a well-needed pot of coffee, Nikki tied the pink robe she was wearing closed and sat down at the kitchen table. With a cop perched outside her cabin on watch, she felt safe enough to relax in her home, but going back out into the public eye was another story altogether. "Where did you wander off to, Hawk?" Nikki whispered.

A knock at the back door answered Nikki's question. Not understanding how, Nikki knew the visitor was Hawk. Standing up, she slowly ran her tired hands through her hair and walked to the back door. "What do you want?" she asked Hawk.

Exhausted from a long night of legwork, still dressed in

the clothes he had been wearing the day before, Hawk looked past Nikki toward the coffee pot. "Can I come in?"

"No," Nikki stated. Folding her arms, she studied Hawk's exhausted face. "Where have you been?"

"Working," Hawk told Nikki in a tone that left no room for any more questions until he was able to soak his system with hot coffee.

Nikki hesitated and then allowed Hawk into the kitchen. "Sit down. I'll pour you a cup of coffee."

Hawk gratefully walked to the kitchen table and plopped his tired body down. Looking at Nikki dressed in a pink robe with her hair a mess appealed to him. Usually, the woman was finely dressed with a dash of makeup that made her appear intelligent and striking—a woman he would have never dared approach for a date. Nikki was out of his league. This woman was far too beautiful for him. But seeing Nikki in morning apparel made Hawk feel as if, maybe, Nikki wasn't so far out of his league, after all. He was seeing the human part of Nikki with all her shields down. "Thanks," he said, taking his cup of coffee from Nikki.

She sat down across from him and slowly sipped at her coffee before speaking. "Why are you protecting the Snowfields?" she finally demanded.

Hawk gulped down his cup of coffee, burning his tongue as he did. "Well," he said, setting the coffee cup down on the table, "it's like this, Nikki. The land the Snowfields own is divided in half, part on the American side and part on the Canadian side, even though on the map it appears to be completely on the American side. Mr. Snowfield is an American citizen, but his wife has Canadian citizenship."

"I'm sorry, Hawk, but I'm not following you," Nikki said, confused.

"I don't want the Canadians in on this," Hawk said simply, "and I don't want to spook the Snowfields into running. Heck, all they have to do is stand near the lake and they're in Canada...I won't be able to touch them. I couldn't risk you spooking them."

"I see," Nikki said and began to fire her artillery at Hawk. Then she paused. The truth was, Hawk was right. After all, he was a detective, and she was only a private citizen tagging along for the ride. He had people to answer to, people who could destroy his job and cast him out on the curb. What did she have to lose? Nothing. "Why didn't you tell me?"

"Look," Hawk said, looking down at his coffee cup, "I don't think the Snowfields killed our John Doe, but I do know they tampered with the suitcase. Before you ask, no, I wasn't able to get any prints off that, but my gut tells me that someone cleaned it out."

"I did see Mr. Snowfield walking back from the lake carrying a shovel yesterday," Nikki told Hawk, taking his coffee cup and refilling it.

"The Snowfields are as cold as ice," Hawk said as he watched Nikki pour coffee into his cup.

"Zach Snowfield isn't mentally ill," she told Hawk, sitting down. "He played you like a fiddle yesterday."

"I know that boy is as sane as anyone else," Hawk said. "I...look, I admit, I lied about him, but I wanted you to stay away from the lodge, okay? After talking to the Snowfields...Mr. Snowfield may be old, but he made it clear that he was going to shoot anyone he saw sneaking around his property. I got worried for you, okay? So hate me."

"I don't hate you," Nikki told Hawk in a soft voice, finally understanding the truth. "Where were you last night?"

"I went to the lodge...and, well, broke the law. I couldn't get a search warrant from the judge, so I trespassed onto private property," Hawk said, shaking his head in exhaustion.

"You think Mr. Snowfield is the owner of the truck?" Nikki asked.

"That was my hunch, but I came up empty-handed. But let me say this, the back of your SUV is smashed pretty good, so the front end of the truck that hit you has to be in pretty bad shape, too," Hawk explained. "The sorry part of this story is that there isn't a truck registered to the Snowfields."

"On the American side," Nikki pointed out to Hawk. "Mr. Snowfield could have driven the truck over the border."

"I thought about that," Hawk said, impressed with Nikki's quick thinking. "Nikki, listen, my hunch is that the Snowfields stole whatever money was in the suitcase. But that still leaves a killer...and a very serious question: Why didn't the killer take the money?"

"Maybe the killer wanted the money to be found?"

Nikki asked and took a sip of her coffee. "Henry Greendale worked for a security firm. He was working in a major bank at the time of his death. His car was stolen by a man who remains a John Doe."

"But why would the killer want our John Doe caught with the money? I can't even find out who the guy is!"

"Maybe the identity of our John Doe, Hawk, was in the suitcase," Nikki suggested.

Hawk stared at Nikki. "You're as brilliant as you are beautiful," he said without worrying if Nikki accepted the compliment or not. "So we need to find the money, which leads us back to the Snowfields."

"What was the name of the security firm Mr. Greendale worked for?" Nikki asked, sidestepping around the Snowfields for a few minutes.

"Prestige Security, why?"

"Well," Nikki said, thinking, "it wouldn't hurt to get a list of all the employees, anyone who knew Mr. Greendale personally and—" Nikki paused.

"What?" Hawk pressed.

"What about his wife? What about Mr. Greendale's wife?"

"They were separated at the time of his death," Hawk told Nikki and then added, "Ah, I see. We need to track down his wife."

Nikki smiled. "Partners?"

"If you get shot, I'll kill you myself," Hawk said, drained his coffee, and then shook Nikki's hand. Standing up, he walked to the back door. "Okay, stay in town today, and I mean it. Tonight we'll sneak back out to the lodge and look around and—"

"Hawk," Nikki said, drawing in a deep breath, "I talked with Zach yesterday. He was the first person into the room." Nikki explained her conversation with Zach to Hawk. "He swears that he didn't touch the suitcase and didn't even step foot back in the room, for that matter."

"Yeah, I kinda figured I was being lied to. It was pretty obvious that the Snowfields had coached that boy into acting stupid, too," Hawk told Nikki. Taking everything in, he focused on what Nikki had said about seeing Mr. Snowfield carrying a shovel back from the lake. "If Mr. Snowfield buried the money—and he probably did—man, it'll be like looking for a needle in a haystack."

"I know," Nikki agreed. "Hawk, I need the list of the members of that women's club that's supposed to be arriving at the lodge. I need the names of all the guests."

"Unless I get a warrant, which I can't—the judge is really being stubborn on this one—I don't see how we can get that list."

Nikki stood up from her chair. "Hawk, I bet ten dollars that Mr. Greendale's wife is a guest on that list."

"I'll find out," Hawk promised. "In the meantime, you stay in town, okay? You put a few gray hairs on my head last night."

"I promise I'll stay in town," Nikki told Hawk. "I have a feeling I'm going to have a cop following me around like a shadow all day, anyway."

"That's right, you are." Hawk smiled and opened the

back door. "I'll be back after dark, and we'll go to the lodge together. I doubt we'll find anything, but maybe?"

"We have to find that money," Nikki warned Hawk. "Without the money, we're sunk."

"I know," Hawk agreed. "See you later," he said and closed the back door.

"It's a date," Nikki smiled.

11

After waking Tori up and taking a hot shower, Nikki dressed in a dark gray dress and walked outside onto her front porch. With her SUV in the shop, she was dependent on Lidia. Spotting a cop car parked across the street, Nikki bit down on her lower lip. "Play it nice for today," she cautioned herself, "and do as Hawk asked. There is no sense in making an old man use you as target practice."

"Who are you talking to?" Tori asked, stepping out onto the front porch.

"Oh, just the voices in my head," Nikki joked, turning around. "No," she said, examining the small t-shirt Tori was wearing. "Come on, honey, back inside."

Twenty minutes later, Tori stepped back onto the front porch wearing a soft pink dress. "I feel funny," she told Nikki in a nervous voice.

"You look beautiful," Nikki beamed. "Now, this is the

way you should always look. Tori, you're a very beautiful young woman."

Tori looked down at the pink pumps Nikki had given her. "No one has ever told me that I'm beautiful before."

"Someday the right man is going to come along and fall in love with your beauty," Nikki promised. "You make sure he falls in love with your heart even more."

"You really think I'll actually fall in love someday?" Tori asked, feeling her cheeks blush bright red.

"I do," Nikki smiled and hugged Tori. "Now, your job today is to consider my offer. I think it would be great if you moved in with me. It's obvious to everyone that you're not happy living with your aunt."

"I'm not," Tori confessed. "Nikki, I...what if you get sick of me and ask me to leave?"

"That will never happen," Nikki promised. "Tori, you're a very special young lady. You don't deserve to be unhappy. I'm not going to promise that living here will be exciting, but you'll be safe and have security. So if you're willing to tolerate me, I think it would be wonderful."

"Me, too," Tori smiled happily. Hearing a car, she looked out at the driveway and saw Lidia pull up. "I hope she likes my dress."

"I'm sure she will and—" Nikki stopped talking when she saw Zach get out of the passenger side of the car. Out of instinct, she eased Tori behind her back and slowly backed up to the open front door. "Inside," she told Tori.

Tori did as Nikki ordered. When she saw Lidia get out of her car and wave an "it's okay" hand at her, she relaxed. "I found him walking. He said he had to speak with you,"

Lidia called out to Nikki as Zach walked up onto the front porch.

"Inside," Nikki said, glancing at the cop car parked across the street. She waved at the cop car in a way that told the officer watching her that everything was okay.

"Yeah, whatever," Zach said, walking through the front door. As soon as he saw Tori, his jaw hit the ground. "Hey again," he said.

"Oh brother," Tori said, but she still blushed at the way Zach was looking at her.

Closing the front door, Nikki approached Zach. "How did you know where I lived?"

Zach looked at Tori and then at Lidia. Lidia folded her arms over a dark blue shirt. "You two ladies lied to me yesterday...cool, I guess."

Nikki examined Zach's black t-shirt and jeans. He looked like the type of guy who knew how to ram someone off a road with a truck. "I want an answer."

"Cool it," Zach told Nikki, "I know what you're getting at. I wasn't the one driving the truck."

"Your grandfather then?" Nikki asked.

Zach walked over to the living room couch and sat down. "Real nice place...too feminine for my taste, though."

"Don't make me hit you over the head with a baseball bat," Lidia warned Zach.

"Cool it, Granny," Zach told Lidia, "I come in peace, you know. I'm here because I want to do the right thing, so get off my back, okay?"

"Doing the right thing means showing respect to your elders," Nikki pointed out to Zach.

"Yeah, okay...sorry," Zach apologized to Lidia.

"You can make it up by helping me at the store later," Lidia told Zach, "and afterward I'll buy you lunch."

"Kinda hungry now," Zach confessed. "I skipped breakfast."

"There's some breakfast food in the kitchen," Nikki told Lidia.

"How do you like your eggs?" Lidia asked Zach.

"Well done...please."

Lidia smiled. "Now see, was that so hard? I can tell that you're going to be just fine, honey. Let Lidia go cook you a good homemade breakfast."

"Uh, sure," Zach said, taken aback by Lidia's sudden surge of warmness toward him.

"I'll help," Tori told Lidia. Looking over her shoulder, she saw Zach nervously put his hands together.

"Okay," Nikki said, sitting down, "what's going on?"

"The old man was the one driving the truck, but don't think for a minute he's stupid."

"The truck is in Canada, isn't it?" Nikki asked.

"Yeah," Zach confessed. "I saw the old man drive the truck up the back trail. Man, I thought he killed you from the damage I saw."

"How did you know your grandfather was coming after me?"

"I heard him talking to the old woman," Zach explained. "I wanted to warn you, but how could I? I almost called the cops, but...that was a red light, too. I felt pretty bad all night. Anyway, I had to make sure you were alive."

"I appreciate that," Nikki told Zach. "Now, tell me what you heard your grandparents talking about."

"The old man saw you leave yesterday," Zach explained. "He grilled me about who you were. I played stupid and said you were just somebody looking for a room, but he saw your license plate. Local plates, not smart, you know."

"I know," Nikki agreed. "Keep going, please."

"Well, your name was in the paper...some hotshot reporter from Atlanta who cracked a pretty big case around here a couple of weeks back."

"I see," Nikki said, "so your grandfather thinks I'm a nosy reporter, then?"

"That's what he told the old lady. He said he was going to scare you off," Zach finished. "But let me tell you, he wasn't happy last night. He was angrier than a wet hornet. I heard him tell the old lady that they had to move fast, whatever that meant."

Nikki nibbled on her lip. "Zach, where do your grandparents think you are right now?"

"They told me to take a hike...go for a walk...in other words, to get lost for a few hours," Zach replied, raising his eyes. "Hey, no sweat, right? I wanted to check on you anyway. I found out where you lived by asking a few people in town. Good thing your friend came along. Man, it's a long walk."

"Okay," Nikki said, grateful for Zach, "here's what I need from you, Zach. I need the names of all the women that are due to arrive at the lodge."

"You mean that women's club?"

Nikki nodded her head. "Please."

"Yeah, sure, I guess I can get you the names."

"I also need you to keep your eyes open and call me," Nikki said, giving Zach the number to her cabin and the store. "Memorize the numbers."

"I got them," Zach said, proud of his memory. "Can I ask you a question?"

"Sure."

"The old man, whatever was in that dead man's suitcase, he stole it, didn't he?" Zach asked.

"I think so, yes."

"I kinda figured he did too, just by the way he forbade me to go back into the room," Zach told Nikki. "What was it, money? What am I asking? The old man has always been a money-hungry wolf."

"Why?" Nikki asked. "The lodge should bring him in quite a bit of income each year."

"The lodge," Zach said, lowering his eyes, "the lodge is a really cool place, you know. I like it. I don't mind the whole living out in the woods like a bear type thing. And yeah, the old man and the old woman are doing pretty good for themselves, if they played by the rules, but..."

"But what?" Nikki asked.

"Oh come on," Zach said, keeping his eyes lowered, "you're the reporter. Put two and two together."

"Drugs?" Nikki asked.

"Let's just say that the lodge isn't for guests only," Zach told Nikki, finally looking up at her. "The dead guy was probably a drug dealer or something, and the old man was more than happy to steal his money. Who knows, maybe the old man killed the guy himself?"

"I don't think so," Nikki assured Zach. "I do believe your grandfather stole whatever was in the dead man's suitcase, which I do believe was money."

"You might as well kiss that money goodbye," Zach told Nikki, standing up from the couch.

"I saw your grandfather walking back from the lake carrying a shovel yesterday," Nikki dared to confess. Patiently, she waited for Zach to react.

Walking to the fireplace, Zach examined the mantel. "That sneaky snake," he finally said. "I knew it...I knew he was up to something. That's why they put me in the lobby. They wanted to keep me grounded inside, and like a dope I played along."

Nikki walked over to Zach and put her hand on his shoulder. "Don't get any funny ideas about finding the money for yourself and then trying to disappear into Canada."

Zach turned his head and looked at Nikki. "You're pretty good at reading people's thoughts."

"Give me your word, okay?"

"No can do," Zach told Nikki, easing toward the front door. "Listen, I'm glad you're alive and all, and I did the right thing by coming here, but I'm not going to promise that if a fortune falls into my hands, I won't split with it."

Instead of going after Zach, Nikki stood still. "So run with stolen money," she told Zach in a disappointed voice, "but you will never be a man, Zach. Real men stand for the truth; cowards take the easy way out."

"Yeah...uh, tell your friend thanks for breakfast, but I gotta run," Zach said, opening the front door.

"Good luck with your life," Nikki told Zach in a voice that struck Zach as if someone punched him in the face.

"What do you mean by that?" he asked.

"You can run away with a dead man's money, but you won't get far, Zach. Inside you'll always be a criminal. And when the money runs out, then what will you do? Steal again...and again...always looking for the easy door to take?"

Zach looked down at the doorknob attached to the front door. "Some people just have to do what's right for themselves. No one cares about me, lady."

"I do," Nikki said.

"I do too," Lidia said, walking into the living room carrying a plate of delicious eggs, turkey bacon, toast, and jam.

"You seem like a nice guy if you want to be," Tori added, holding a cup of coffee. Walking up to Zach, she reached out with the cup of coffee. "Friends matter," she smiled.

Zach looked from Tori to Lidia, and then back at Nikki. "Man," he groaned, "a bunch of women melting me down like butter on a hot stove. Yeah, sure," he said, closing the front door, "I'll live like a poor man the rest of my life if it makes you three happy."

"What would make me happy is knowing how you know where your grandfather buried the money," Nikki told Zach, "but for now, you need to eat."

"Come on, honey," Lidia smiled at Zach and walked him into the kitchen.

"He's pretty beaten down, isn't he?" Tori asked Nikki.

"If I had an extra guest room I would give it to him," Nikki answered. Putting her arm around Tori, she walked into the kitchen. A long day awaited her, but at least she had a secret weapon. Maybe she and Hawk wouldn't come up empty-handed after all.

In the distance, clouds began to form. A dangerous storm was brewing.

12

Zach eased in through the front door of the lobby. He was sweaty from walking three miles to the lodge after Lidia dropped him off. That had been Nikki's idea, because she wanted Zach to return to the lodge appearing as if he had been out walking. All he wanted was a glass of cold water. Instead, he was met by a mean-faced old man wearing a brown buttoned shirt tucked into a pair of old jeans. "Where have you been, boy?"

"Around," Zach fired back, shoving his hands down into the pockets of his jeans. "You told me to get lost, remember?"

Jason Snowfield glared at Zach with angry eyes. "You were gone too long."

"Oh, back off," Zach said, standing his ground, "I met this chick on the side of the road," he lied. "She was driving up into Canada with another cute chick. I took them down the old back trail to Frostline Lake."

Jason examined Zach's sweaty face. It wasn't unlike his grandson to meet up with strange girls and sweet-talk them for every penny they owned. "Norma is in town. Watch the lobby for me. I have business to tend to out on the property," he ordered Zach, buying into the lie hook, line, and sinker.

"Why did she go into town?" Zach asked, walking to the front counter. To make sure his question didn't seem suspicious, he added, "I wouldn't have minded a break from this rat hole."

Jason ignored Zach's insult. He had far too much on his mind. Dealing with a smart mouth brat took too much time and energy. "Norma went into town to ask around about that nosy reporter. If you see her back here, you come get me, you hear?"

"Sure," Zach said, leaning against the front counter, "I'll run quick like a bunny, Gramps. In the meantime, my reward is all the wonderful trees to stare at," he finished.

Jason pointed a cold finger at Zach. "Don't push it, boy," he warned and hurried outside.

Zach rolled his eyes and walked behind the front counter. Sitting down at the check-in desk he began to shuffle through papers. "All right, lady," he said, referring to Nikki, "let's see if I can play your game, play everybody's game."

Walking away from the front lobby, Jason Snowfield took an open trail leading to the lake. Walking past beautiful trees playing in a soft breeze, he kept his face hard and focused. He had buried the stolen money in a safe location, but what worried him was one simple fact: A man had been killed, and the killer was still loose. Not sure if the killer wanted the money or not, Jason worried that the lodge was being watched by hidden eyes. Pausing on the trail, he searched the landscape for any sign of human eyes. Only the sound of the breeze playing in the trees answered back. "You're around," Jason said in an angry but worried voice, "I know you're watching."

Reaching the water's edge, he once again paused. The lake stood before him, open, clear, deep, and breathtakingly beautiful. He looked toward the wooden dock and counted the paddle boats and canoes. Every one of them was accounted for. The waters of the lake gently swayed. Soft ripples cruised the top of the lake like sleepy old men searching for shade to nap in. For a few minutes, Jason forgot about his worries as old memories strolled into his mind. Memories of being young and taking cold swims in the lake. Life was good then...good until criminals forced his lodge to be a go-between station for gun-runners. But now he had the money. He and Norma could leave the lodge and vanish without ever being found. "You can't track cash," Jason whispered.

"Can't you?" a voice asked.

Startled, Jason swung around. The last thing he saw was a hand swinging a hammer at his head, and then the world went dark.

13

In town, Nikki gave free samples of her famous peppermint chocolate to the customers in her store. Periodically checking the cow-shaped clock hanging on the back wall, she waited anxiously for closing time. She didn't want to put Zach in a precarious situation, so she had asked him to leave the guest list hidden in one of the canoes at the lake's edge. "The blue canoe," Zach had told her. Also, after eating breakfast, Zach had confessed that he believed his grandfather had buried the money in a cave at the far back of the property. Of course, that confession didn't come without strings. Tori now owed Zach a date.

"Thank you, come again," Nikki smiled and waved at a middle-aged couple wearing tan shirts. The couple waved back, leaving with a bag stuffed full of chocolates that had cost them a small fortune.

"Almost closing time," Lidia told Nikki, watching the couple leave the store. "Whew, what a morning and afternoon! We're almost completely sold out. I checked the cooler, too, and would you believe we're running low?"

"A new shipment will be arriving tomorrow, and I'll find time to make some more homemade chocolates," Nikki told Lidia as she waved for Tori to lock the front door. Taking a deep breath of air filled with chocolate, Nikki slowly exhaled. "We'll close twenty minutes early, girls," she said. "I'm bushed."

"I am, too," Lidia said gratefully. "My feet are barking. Herbert is grilling steaks tonight. I'm going to go eat, soak my feet, do a crossword or two, and go to bed."

"You promised to take me to my aunt's house first," Tori reminded Lidia in a nervous voice. "I'll pack as quickly as I can. I promise."

"You take your time, honey," Lidia told Tori and patted her hand. "Just as long as this old woman's backside is sitting down, I'll be fine."

"Oh," Nikki said and hurried to her purse. Returning with her house key, she handed it to Tori. "I'm not sure what time I'll be back. Hawk and I are going out to the lodge to look around tonight. You can leave the back door unlocked. We'll get an extra key made tomorrow."

Tori looked at the house key. For once in her life, she felt welcomed and loved. Taking the key from Nikki, she thanked her. "I promise to stay out of your hair."

"If you do that then I promise to get into yours," Nikki joked. "Sweetie, my cabin is your cabin. You make it into your home, and that's an order. Don't tip-toe around and think you have to walk on eggshells, okay?"

"Okay," Tori promised. "I guess I'll go sweep."

Hearing someone knock at the front door, Lidia sighed. "Let me see who that is."

"It's Hawk," Nikki said, not understanding how she knew. Shaking her head, she tried to explain the funny feeling that entered her stomach as soon as she heard Hawk knock on the front door.

Lidia unlocked the front door and let him in. "Thank you," he said, immediately overpowered by the smell of chocolate. He liked Nikki's store. The place was cozy and quaint, simple but inviting. "Got time to talk?"

"I'll start the paperwork," Lidia told Nikki.

"What have you found out?" Nikki asked Hawk, easing him toward the front door.

"Veronica Greendale is what," Hawk informed Nikki, "Greendale's wife."

Nikki nodded. "Well, don't keep me in the dark—out with it!"

"Henry Greendale suspected that his wife was...well, fooling around on him. So he hired a private investigator, someone he knew in his own security firm."

"How did you find this out?" Nikki asked in a curious voice.

"I made some calls," Hawk replied. "So it turns out that Mrs. Greendale is stepping out on the side." Hawk pulled a photo out of his front pocket. "Look familiar?"

"Our John Doe," Nikki said, staring at a photo of a woman with grayish-red hair sitting at a table and sipping wine with the man found dead at Elk Horn Lodge the day before.

"The women's club coming our way? Guess where they are coming from, and guess who's a member."

"Atlanta, Georgia," Nikki answered. She felt excitement burst through her veins like hot lava. But then she began to wonder about something. "Wait, why come here with a women's club? Why not just come alone and then escape over the border?"

"Some very prominent women are members of that women's club," Hawk explained. "I managed to get some names. It seems like Mrs. Greendale isn't who we think she is."

Nikki attempted to follow Hawk. "I don't quite understand what you—" And then she understood. Feeling a light bulb go off in her head, she slowly nodded. Focusing her eyes back on the photo, she looked hard at Veronica Greendale. "She's a killer."

"No, I don't think so. Our John Doe was the killer," he explained. "That's why I can't find anything on him. Now here is where things get interesting. I think Henry Greendale was catching onto something he wasn't supposed to—maybe at the bank his firm assigned him to—and he was killed. I think Mrs. Greendale paid our John Doe to kill her husband, but something went wrong, and the guy had to get out of town and fast."

"What went wrong?"

Hawk shrugged his shoulders. "I'm not saying anything did, but a sloppy trail was left."

"Go on," Nikki told Hawk.

"The driver's license leads me to believe that our John Doe needed a false identity to cross into Canada. My guess is the photos of Mrs. Greendale sipping wine with Mr. Six Feet Under are probably times they met in order to agree on a price and time to kill her husband."

"But there are some loose ends," Nikki pointed out. "Why did the driver's license have Mr. Greendale's address on it?"

"Nikki, I don't know. I'm telling you what I have so far. We have a connection between Greendale's wife and our John Doe along with a lot of speculative ideas. What we don't have is the money."

"Hawk," Nikki said, nodding her head, "you said some very important women are members of the women's club and due to arrive here, right?"

"Some of Atlanta's finest," Hawk confirmed.

"Is it possible Mrs. Greendale is luring them here to be killed?"

"I considered that. The reservation was made two weeks before Henry Greendale was killed, about the same time he started having his wife investigated," Hawk explained. "Nikki, when that woman gets here, we have to let her lead us to the killer."

"I agree," Nikki told Hawk. "In the meantime, we have to find the money." Nikki went into detail about the cave where Zach believed his grandfather had buried the money. "He's not a bad kid, Hawk. He just needs someone like you, a good man, to take time with him."

"Yeah," Hawk said and rubbed the back of his neck, "I'm not too good with the younger generation, Nikki. Anyways, listen, I'm going to grab a bite to eat and then grab a few hours of sleep. I'll pick you up around midnight, okay?"

"I'll be waiting," Nikki promised. She could see that he was completely exhausted. "Get some rest."

"I will," Hawk replied, giving Nikki a look that clearly warned her to stay in town. "Midnight, got it?"

"I got it, I got it," Nikki said, throwing her hands up into the air. "Now will you go get some rest before you fall over?"

"One more thing," Hawk pointed out. "Rumors were floating around Atlanta that she was becoming very cozy with the mayor. I think that's who Greendale thought his wife was stepping out with. I talked with the mayor, and he told me that it was true—he and Mrs. Greendale did have a few drinks together, but when things started to turn serious, he dropped her like a hot rock. Soon after, Mrs. Greendale joined the women's club, the same club the mayor's wife attends."

"Very interesting," Nikki replied. "When I lived and worked in Atlanta, I was kinda given a black mark at City Hall, so I never got much information from the mayor's office. It was always known the mayor was a man with wandering eyes and that his wife was only a 'political' wife. Men like that disgust me, so I never wasted my time on him."

"Whatever is going on," Hawk told Nikki, "until it ends, the body count will rise unless we stop it. I don't have all the answers yet, and I admit, I am stuck over our John Doe having a driver's license with the same address as Henry Greendale, but I'm sure the answers will come. See you later, okay? Oh, and I finally got the autopsy report—heart attack. Dead end on that one."

Nikki let Hawk out and locked the door behind him. The new information had her mind running around a maze, bumping into dead ends here, making a little progress there. Nibbling on her lip again, she walked into the back office and leaned against the wall. "Lidia?"

Lidia held up her right hand. She was counting the cash drawer down. "Don't make me lose count," she begged.

Nikki nodded her head and waited. Why would a dead man have the address of another dead man on a fake driver's license, she wondered? And if the John Doe found at the lodge was a professional killer hired by Mrs. Greendale, why would he escape Atlanta with her husband's car and a fake driver's license with her husband's home address on it? Confused, Nikki watched Lidia fill out a bank deposit slip. "All done?"

"All done," Lidia said, placing the deposit slip into a bank bag holding the daily sales cash. Closing the bag, she looked up at Nikki. "What did Hawk want?"

"He had some new information on the case," Nikki told Lidia and slowly explained about the photo, adding in the new information as carefully as she possibly could.

"Oh dear," Lidia said, feeling as if someone punched her in the stomach. "My, this is serious. And you believe this Mrs. Greendale woman is luring those poor women here to kill them?"

"Maybe not all of them. I just wonder if she knows if her hired killer is dead. If she does, she might not even show up…or cancel the reservation altogether. Hawk also believes something went wrong in Atlanta, and the killer had to leave town fast. I wonder…"

"Wonder what?" Lidia asked, regretting that she had to ask.

"Well," Nikki said, leaning up against the wall, "I wonder if the bank Henry Greendale's firm assigned him to has anything to do with this. I'm sure the suitcase I saw in the room at the lodge had been filled with money. If Mrs. Greendale paid a killer to murder her husband, how did she get the money?"

"Honey, you're chasing your tail," Lidia pointed out.

"Maybe, but maybe…just maybe, Henry Greendale isn't dead," Nikki told Lidia.

Lidia felt her blood turn cold. The idea of a dead man walking around spooked her to the bone. "Honey, I don't like horror movies. I don't even like bug spray commercials, okay? The last thing I need to think about when I'm falling asleep is a glowing body walking around in these woods."

"What I mean is," Nikki corrected herself, "maybe Henry Greendale wasn't killed after all. Maybe the killer murdered someone else, set the house on fire, and then realized that his victim was still alive, and that's why he had to leave Atlanta in haste."

"You would know better than me," Lidia admitted. Standing up with the bank deposit bag, she walked over to Nikki. "I'm going to the bank, help Tori get situated, and then go spend time with my grumpy husband who still thinks you're a nut. Now, since I have the only car, you're coming with me. I know you're up to something because you gave Tori your house key. If you refuse to come with me, I'm going to call Hawk."

"Beats walking," Nikki caved in, reading the seriousness in Lidia's eyes. Unable to break away from the powerful stare of a woman who loved her like a mother, Nikki confessed her intentions. "Okay, fine, Mrs. Snowfield has been asking people about me today. The new girl over at the paper came in and told me this earlier. I was going to see if I could locate her in town."

"When I walked down to the Jukebox to get us a burger earlier, I saw a woman standing across the street watching the store," Lidia told Nikki. "Now listen, dear, for now, go home. You and Hawk are going to play spies tonight anyway, so do this old lady a favor, go home and give me peace of mind for now."

"Okay," Nikki promised. "I guess if the Snowfields want to meet me badly enough, they will. After all, Mr. Snowfield has already said hello."

14

Nikki was back at her cabin a few hours later, standing on her front porch and waving goodbye to Lidia. Inside, Tori was in her room, unpacking her belongings. Yawning, Nikki closed the front door and walked into the kitchen. Deciding on coffee, she made a fresh pot and sat down at the kitchen table.

As Nikki drank her coffee, Norma Snowfield started to become worried about her husband. Pulling her long gray hair into a ponytail, she walked out of the lobby and headed toward the lake. The day was growing tired, and night was beginning to pull the light of the sun down below the horizon. Norma always liked the nighttime. She especially liked it when it rained. And the way the sky was looking overhead, a good storm was brewing. It would be raining by midnight, she guessed. "Jason, where are you?"

she called out as she neared the lake. With the wind picking up from the approaching storm, the lake was slowly beginning to turn choppy. Norma heard the paddle boats and canoes bumping against each other.

Looking up into a dark gray sky, she became even more worried. It wasn't like Jason to stay out too long. Even when he had numerous chores to do, he always checked in with her at least every hour. "Jason?" she called out again, looking around. "That darn man and his fool ideas," she said, thinking about the stolen money, "why didn't he leave that money alone?"

"That's a very good question," a voice said.

Nearly jumping out of her skin, Norma spun around as fast as she could. The last thing the wife of Jason Snowfield saw was the same hammer that killed her husband before it smashed down onto her head. Throwing the hammer into the deep lake, the killer grabbed Norma's body and pulled it into a small but wide cave. Dropping the body onto the damp earth, the killer squatted down with narrowed eyes. "Now we wait."

"So sweet," Nikki said, looking down at Tori. Sleeping peacefully with a blue sheet wrapped around her, Tori let out a little snore. "Sweet baby." Bending down, Nikki wiped Tori's bangs out of her eyes and then kissed her forehead. "Sleep well."

Closing the door to the guest room, she rejoined Hawk in the living room. "Tori is asleep."

Listening to the heavy rainfall outside the cabin, Hawk debated on whether to take a trip out to the lodge or wait. "With this storm—"

"We're going to the lodge," Nikki interrupted. Picking up a dark green raincoat she had laid across the arm of the chair, Nikki used her eyes to order Hawk to get up from the couch. "The rain will help hide us," she said, putting on the raincoat.

"Stubborn," Hawk said, walking to the front door and yanking his black raincoat off the wooden coat rack that was, like everything else in the cabin, very stylish. Having no sense of style whatsoever, Hawk wondered how Nikki made her cabin appear stylish and intelligent yet at the same time inviting and welcoming. "All right, let's go, Nancy Drew."

"Watch it," Nikki warned Hawk as she elbowed him in the stomach. Opening the front door, she peered out into a dark and stormy night. Every mystery novel that she had ever read came alive in her imagination. Dark and stormy nights were what brought true mysteries to life. In her mind she saw an insane Dr. Frankenstein yelling 'It's alive...it's alive!' while standing in a creepy lab in some old castle. "Perfect night."

"Yeah," Hawk said, closing the front door behind Nikki, "all we need now is a picnic basket and some cheese."

"Funny," Nikki said and elbowed him in the stomach again. "Are you sure your cop friend won't leave Tori?"

"Max knows his orders," Hawk assured Nikki. He peered out into the rain and spotted a parked cop car across the street. "He's probably eating a donut and listening to the game."

Feeling a powerful gust of wind spray rain in her face, Nikki raised her hands up to her eyes. Not wasting another second, she ran off the porch and hurried to Hawk's jeep. Hawk shook his head and followed after Nikki. Crawling up into the driver's seat, he buckled up and slowly backed out of the driveway. "Don't expect me to break any speed limits."

"Better safe than sorry," Nikki agreed, watching the windshield wipers fight with the rain. Leaning forward, she pushed the defrost button. "So I was doing some thinking, and I think I know why the address on our John Doe's fake license matched the real address of Henry Greendale."

"I'm all ears, because I'm coming up short," Hawk said, cautiously maneuvering the jeep through the storm. "I can barely see..."

"Go slow," Nikki told Hawk and then began to explain her theory. "I began to wonder if Henry Greendale's real name was Jack Johnson. I was thinking about the security firm he worked for, so I spent some time on the internet doing some research."

"The security firm is legitimate. I checked."

"Maybe it is on the outside," Nikki pointed out, feeling a strong gust of wind rock the jeep. "Did you know the security firm came under investigation for hiring ex-cons?"

"No, I didn't," Hawk said and focused his attention on Nikki while allowing his instinct to take over the driving.

"I called my detective friend in Atlanta and had him run the name Jack Johnson through the Federal Prison System

Database. I also had him email an actual photo of Mr. Greendale. Mr. Greendale and Mr. Johnson have the same face. And," Nikki emphasized, "as it turns out, Mr. Greendale was sent to prison for quite a long time for bank robbery in the early 1990s. Then, strangely enough, he was allowed an early parole and shortly after began working for the security firm in Atlanta. He was paroled from—drum roll, please—a prison in upstate New York."

"Remind me to marry you," Hawk said, impressed. "What else you got?"

"Four years later, Mr. Greendale, or should I say Mr. Johnson, married his current wife, who also happens to be an ex-con."

"Yeah, I have her background. I ran it. I was going to go into that tomorrow. She was also released from a women's prison in upstate New York."

Nikki patted Hawk's arm. "Now you don't have to worry about telling me," she said, watching Hawk reach a stop sign and slow to a stop. "Mrs. Greendale was found guilty of forgery. Strangely enough, the same security firm that hired Mr. Johnson once employed his wife. I'm assuming that's where they met. So, where does that leave us? Well, Mr. Johnson is assigned to a bank. He's a thief, remember. So what does he start doing? He starts stealing...but not just from the bank, but from the security firm who, in my opinion, created Mr. Johnson's new identity."

"Mr. Greendale."

"Yes," Nikki told Hawk, feeling the jeep move through the four-way stop as the tires worked through a deep puddle. "Hawk, in my opinion, the security firm put Mr. Johnson in a position that would allow him to steal millions from a very powerful bank."

"But Mr. Johnson starts stealing money he shouldn't?"

"Yes, and his wife finds out. She comes up with a plan," Nikki continued. "Kill her husband when the time is right. Only something goes wrong."

"What?"

"Well, the security firm hired our John Doe to kill Mr. Johnson, I'm sure of that. They must have found out he was stealing from them. That's why the address on the driver's license matches up. Kill the real man, have another man keep him alive on paper. Somewhere down the line, our John Doe starts liking Mrs. Greendale, who, due to her past prison record, is determined to become part of the high society crowd. Somehow this woman found out her husband was stealing money...she can't have him tarnishing her reputation, right? After all, she's already struck out with the mayor."

"I'm all ears, Nikki, don't stop now."

"I'm sure the security firm Mr. Johnson worked for wanted both him and his wife dead, but our John Doe, well, has other ideas. Now here is where I get off into some muddy water, so what I'm about to imply isn't fact."

"Jump in the deep end."

"Mr. Johnson's body was supposedly found burned up in a house fire, right? But let's say he somehow escapes. Let's assume our John Doe thinks he's dead but then finds out he's not. So he leaves Atlanta—he's in some serious hot water because he went against his employer."

"Which means he didn't kill Mr. Johnson the way he was ordered to?"

"Exactly," Nikki said, "so he makes haste. But, that leaves Mrs. Greendale. She's still alive. Which made me start thinking about the women's club."

"Throw it at me," Hawk told Nikki, pushing the jeep through another deep puddle. "We may not get back without a boat."

Nikki agreed. "The roads are low and flood easily."

"So what about the women's club?"

"Mrs. Greendale needs to stay alive, right? If her new Romeo ran scared, she must be worried. I'm not certain if she knows her husband is still alive or not, but I am certain if our John Doe hurried to the lodge, Mrs. Greendale isn't sitting in Atlanta doing her nails. She and John Doe agreed to meet at the lodge."

"With her husband dead—or presumed dead—the security firm backs off of her because it can't look too suspicious, right?"

"Possibly," Nikki said, "and Mrs. Greendale uses her membership to guard her against further harm. What I mean is, she goes to the mayor, who wants his wife dead."

"Okay, you just lost me."

"It's a chessboard," Nikki explained. "Mrs. Greendale kills the mayor's wife, and the mayor does her a favor—you rub my back, I rub yours. I know you said he dropped her like a hot rock, but that could have been for outward purposes. In the meantime, Mrs. Greendale has to get rid of her husband, who is threatening to ruin her reputation if he gets caught stealing, so what does she do? She romances the hitman who was sent to kill her, too."

"And the mayor's wife is still coming to the lodge; Mrs. Greendale will be where our John Doe will be waiting for her. He kills the mayor's wife, Mrs. Greendale kills him, she returns back to Atlanta and what...gets put on a pedestal?"

"Something like that," Nikki agreed. "I know my theory is merely speculation, but it's all I have to go on. I guess our John Doe didn't know that Mrs. Greendale was planning on killing him. That explains why she chose a place so close to the border, too. Just in case anything went wrong, she could make her escape with the money she paid John Doe to kill her husband...money Mr. Johnson stole from the bank."

"I think you've hit the ball out of the park," Hawk told Nikki. "So the only question is, who did our John Doe really kill in Atlanta?"

"Who knows? My guess is Mr. Johnson knew he was about to be killed and was prepared," Nikki said. "I think Mr. Johnson is hanging around the lodge waiting for his wife to arrive. I also think he knows who the killer is. My guess, Hawk, is that after he kills his wife, he'll leave us a clue as to who John Doe is."

"We're not going to let him kill his wife."

"I hope not," Nikki agreed. "The women's group is due to arrive tomorrow. Zach called me from the lodge. He told me the reservation was pushed up."

Hawk looked at Nikki and then focused back on the road. "And you were going to tell me this when?"

"Just now," Nikki played innocent.

Hawk pressed down a little harder on the gas. "Hold on," he said, gripping the steering wheel harder.

Nikki leaned back in her seat and grew silent. Watching Hawk speed through dark, wet streets and then through town, she felt as if she were in one of her favorite mystery novels. Even though she was scared out of her wits, she was also excited to the core. She was sitting next to a man who encouraged her to solve crimes instead of being married to a man who refused to support her career at all. Looking at Hawk, she saw a man who was slowly working his way into her heart.

Hawk caught Nikki looking at him. Smiling, he nudged her with his elbow. "What are you looking at?" he asked.

"You have a freckle on your nose." Nikki smiled and looked away.

"I guess I do," Hawk chuckled to himself and then became serious. "When we get to the lodge, you stay at my side, do you hear me? I have my gun, and I'm going to shoot at the first person who threatens your life. I don't need you roaming off, understand?"

"Understand, boss." Nikki saluted Hawk.

"I'm serious, Nikki. We're going to search for the money, and that's it. Tomorrow, after this storm passes, we'll go back out to the lodge and wait for Mrs. Greendale to arrive."

"I understand," Nikki said and apologized.

15

Forty minutes later, Hawk killed the headlights on his jeep, pulled over to the side of the road and parked between a thick pair of trees. "Okay," he said, "the lake is northeast of here about a mile. We're going through the woods and staying out of sight. I don't need Mr. Snowfield using my head as a target tonight."

Nikki nodded. Following Hawk out of the jeep, she stared into the wet darkness. The mystery novels she read never informed her that darkness—real darkness, soaked with rain—somehow empowered a killer and weakened the innocent. Feeling a strange fear grip her stomach, she eased closer to Hawk as strong winds ripped at her hair. "I'm ready," she hollered over the winds.

"Let's go," Hawk hollered, backhanding Nikki a flashlight he had retrieved from the glove compartment. "Don't turn on the flashlight until we reach the cave."

"Okay," Nikki hollered.

Slowly, she and Hawk began to trek through the dark

woods, one wet step at a time, as heavy rain and powerful winds attacked them. Keeping his head low and lifting his left elbow to shield his eyes, Hawk used his right hand to withdraw his service pistol from the holster attached to his belt. He had both humans and animals to worry about. The last thing he needed was to walk up on a bear. Looking over his shoulder, he saw Nikki fighting against the storm. "Not much farther!" he yelled.

"You sure you know the way?" Nikki hollered over the winds.

"If I don't, we can always swim back to town," Hawk answered.

Holding onto Hawk's shoulder, Nikki cautiously followed him through the dark woods, bypassing wet trees and heavy brush. And then, suddenly, the lake appeared like a dark smudge on the ground. Hearing the paddle boats and canoes crashing against each other, Nikki paused. "The cave should be that way," she pointed, attempting to catch her sense of direction. "It's so dark...I can't really tell."

"I know where the cave is. Come on." Reaching behind him, Hawk took Nikki's left hand. Following the lake around to the north end, he stopped and studied the woods. Nodding his head, he moved farther north into the woods. But before he could get too far, a dark shadow darted from behind a tree and started to run toward the lake. "Stop," Hawk yelled and fired a warning shot into the air.

"Don't shoot," Zach yelled, throwing his hands into the air.

"Zach?" Nikki hollered. "Hawk, that's Zach."

Grabbing Nikki's hand again, Hawk jogged over to Zach. "What are you doing out here?" he demanded.

"They're...dead...both of them," Zach said, violently shaking from fear. Soaking wet from the rain, he looked at Nikki. Nikki activated the flashlight and aimed it at Zach's face.

"Who is dead?" Hawk ordered Zach to talk.

"My grandparents. Their bodies are in the cave," Zach said in a shaky voice. "It got dark. They were missing, so I went out and looked for them, you know?"

"Zach," Nikki yelled over the wind, "everything is all right now. No one is going to hurt you."

Hawk read the fear in Zach's face. The young man was scared stiff. "Son," he said in a loud, calm voice, "you better stay with us instead. There's a killer loose."

"I can't go back into that cave," Zach yelled and started backing up. "You can arrest me and throw away the key. I can't see them like that again."

Hawk pulled his cell phone out of his pocket and raised it in the air. "No signal. I need to call this in from the lodge."

"Phones are out," Zach informed Hawk, blocking rain from his face.

Forced to make a difficult choice, Hawk decided to lead Nikki and Zach back to the lodge. "Okay, back to the lodge," Hawk yelled and grabbed Nikki's hand. Looking over his shoulder into the dark woods, Hawk felt deadly eyes watching him. Nikki followed Hawk's eyes into the darkness. Somewhere in the darkness, she felt, a killer was grinning at her.

16

Hawk locked the lobby door behind them as Nikki walked Zach behind the front counter and helped him sit down. Looking around, the first thing Hawk noticed was a door behind the front counter that opened up into a short hallway leading to a laundry and utility room. A wooden door stood solo in the middle of the hallway, allowing access to the second-floor apartment. "Lock that door," Hawk told Nikki.

Zach reached into his wet pants pocket and pulled out a set of keys. "You have to use a key," he said. With shaky hands, he managed to identify the correct key.

Nikki quickly inserted the key into the lock and activated the deadbolt. "What are you thinking?" she asked Hawk, holding onto the keys.

"Wait until morning," Hawk replied, rechecking the lock on the lobby door. "Son," he said, turning his attention back to Zach, "tell me what you saw."

"The old man, he took the money," Zach confessed to

Hawk, and as calmly as he could, he explained how he had found his grandfather's body. "He buried that money in the cave, I bet my life on it. I figured that's where he and the old lady probably were. I was right, but they were...dead. It looked like someone took a hammer to their heads."

"Would make sense," Nikki told Hawk, "no gunshots. A hammer is easy to get rid of."

"Jack Johnson is out there killing people, and I'm trapping myself in here," Hawk said, feeling anger boil in his chest.

Nikki walked over to Hawk and rubbed his shoulder. "It's not your fault, Hawk. We'll catch him. He's sure to go after Mrs. Greendale when she arrives tomorrow."

"I didn't tell you, did I?" Zach asked, forcing his legs to work. Standing up he looked directly at Nikki.

"Tell me what?"

"The reservation was canceled," Zach told Nikki. "I got a call about three hours ago. Some woman who sounded real snotty called and canceled the reservation. She didn't say why, either. That was another reason I went looking for my grandparents. I knew the old man was going to hit the roof."

Hawk shot Nikki a confused glance. "What's going on?" he asked Nikki.

Nikki shrugged her shoulders. "I wish I knew."

Before Hawk could speak, the lobby phone sitting behind the front counter rang. Zach ran to the phone and looked down. "What? This can't be right."

"What?" Hawk asked, running behind the front counter.

"The call is coming from the Deep Woods room...it's an

in-house call," Zach explained. "Someone is in the Deep Woods room. Even with the outside phone line out, you can still make in-house calls."

"Stay here," Hawk ordered Nikki and Zach. "This could be a trap."

"No," Nikki objected. She followed Hawk to the lobby door. "We're partners, remember?"

"I'm not staying here alone," Zach said, running up to Nikki.

"Oh, good grief," Hawk complained. "All right, come on, but stay right behind me. If any shooting starts, just duck and cover."

Nikki nodded. Zach hesitated. The thought of being shot at didn't thrill him. After seeing his grandparents dead, he wasn't too anxious to join them. "I think I'll stay here in the lobby."

"Okay," Nikki told Zach, "lock the door behind us, and don't open it for anyone."

Zach focused his attention on the ringing phone. "Yeah, sure," he said.

"Let's go," Hawk said. Unlocking the lobby door, he prepared his gun, and then, with courage only a real cop possessed, he yanked the door open and ran out into the storm. Nikki followed behind like a faithful wife daring the dangers of death in order to remain united with her husband even though she was absolutely terrified. "Stay close behind me," Hawk hollered, hugging the outside of the lobby with his back. With his gun at the ready, he eased to the edge of the lobby and scanned the guest walkway leading down to the rooms. "Clear," he told Nikki.

"I'm right behind you," Nikki told Hawk, shielding her face from the rain and powerful winds. Grateful that the power was still functioning, she looked up at the set of flood lights mounted on the front corner of the lobby. Even though the lights made them an easy target, Nikki felt grateful for them. Knowing that two dead bodies were lying in a creepy cave in absolute darkness sent icy chills through her body. Following Hawk around the corner, she planted her feet on a pebbled walkway lined with dim but confident overhead lights hanging from the wooden roof. "Are you okay?" she asked when Hawk paused in his approach to the Deep Woods room.

"Here," Hawk said. Kneeling down, he pulled a gun from an ankle holster. "This is an easy 9mm C-9 Model Luger," he explained, clicking the gun's safety off and placing it in Nikki's right hand. "Don't hesitate, just shoot."

Nikki looked down at the gun. Familiar with firearms to a degree, she felt confident enough to defend herself with the Luger. "I won't hesitate," she promised Hawk.

Without saying another word, Hawk nodded, eased his way down to the Deep Woods room, motioned for Nikki to press her back up against the outside wall, and then, with all his might, kicked the door open and charged in. Nikki bravely followed. But instead of finding a dangerous murderer lurking in the shadows, waiting to pronounce death on two innocent people, she and Hawk found a woman tied and gagged, lying on the floor with the room phone beside her.

"I know that woman!" Nikki yelled, slamming the door

shut behind her. "That's the mayor's wife. I've seen her before at press conferences."

Hawk ordered Nikki to untie the woman as he moved to the window in the room. Slowly, he pulled back the edge of a green curtain and peered out into the night. "Hurry it up," he told Nikki.

Kneeling down beside the woman, who was in her late fifties with short black hair, Nikki placed the gun onto the floor and quickly began to untie the thin ropes wrapped around the woman's wrists and ankles. "Goodness, these knots are tough," she told Hawk. Taking her right hand, she pulled a piece of gray duct tape from the woman's mouth and then carefully removed a wadded up washcloth from between her teeth.

"Please, she's going to kill me!" the woman begged in sheer panic. "I don't know why...everything was going according to schedule. We stopped in a small town outside of Albany, New York to rest. I was in my room. The next thing I remember, a hand grabbed my face and I went unconscious and woke up here."

"Probably chloroform," Hawk pointed out. "Ma'am, who is this woman?"

"Veronica Greendale. My name is Amanda Dennington. Please, you have to help me."

"Mrs. Dennington, we're here to help," Nikki assured the frightened woman. "Can you tell us where Mrs. Greendale went? Why did she leave you alone?"

"I really don't know," Amanda said, watching Nikki return to the knots. "I woke up tied up. Veronica was standing at the window, looking out—like he is doing. She had a knife in her hand. And then, all of a sudden, she ran outside. That's when I managed to kick the phone over."

"Ma'am," Hawk said, "the reservation your group arranged—"

"Veronica arranged this trip," Amanda interrupted Hawk. "I had my concerns, but my husband convinced me to allow her to prove her skills to become more welcome in the women's club...on probation, of course."

Hawk looked at Nikki. "You're good," he told her.

"Did Mrs. Greendale say anything to you?" Nikki asked, fighting with the knots.

Amanda nodded her head. "She kept telling me that she was going to become the most powerful woman in Atlanta and use me as an example. I always knew that woman was foul."

"Did she say anything else?" Nikki asked, managing to untie one knot.

"Something about how time was running out," Amanda explained, slowly calming down. "I noticed a change in her behavior when she made a call."

"Where?" Hawk asked. "When did she make this call?"

"This morning," Amanda explained. "Veronica called this establishment. I must say, her entire demeanor changed afterward. We were preparing to leave the hotel we had rested at...perhaps it was seven in the morning. Around, oh, five, Veronica insisted we stop and rest, claiming she was suffering from a headache."

"I see," Nikki said, managing to untie a second knot. "After you stopped, Veronica kidnapped you and brought you here, after she canceled the reservation."

"People will be searching for me," Amanda insisted. "I will see that woman behind bars for the rest of her life."

Still peering out into the storm, Hawk whistled at Nikki. "We have company," he said and rushed away from the window. "Ma'am," he said, lifting Amanda back into the bed and then snatching up the phone and setting it back into place, "act dumb. Nikki put the gag back on."

Moving as quickly as she could, Nikki replaced the gag and then ran into the bathroom with Hawk, closing the door halfway. Seconds later, the door to the room opened. "Get in there," a man said, shoving a woman across the threshold.

"We can work this out!" Mrs. Greendale pleaded. "Jack, I'm sorry, you have to believe me. I—"

"Shut up!" a man in his mid-fifties roared. The man, Nikki saw, peeping through the bathroom door, didn't look like any killer she had ever seen. He was pleasant-looking, like someone she might see browsing around in her store, trying to pick out some chocolate for his wife. Nikki watched the man shake rain off the clear plastic poncho he was wearing over a brown suit and then aim the gun in his hand at his wife. She watched the man's face transform from pleasant into lethal.

"Please," Veronica Greendale pleaded, dropping down to her knees. With tears streaming from her eyes, she begged for her life.

"You tried to kill me mere minutes ago, and now you want me to spare your life," Jack Johnson told his wife. "And look at her—you bring this woman here to murder her in order to marry the mayor of our fair city."

"It's all political, Jack," Veronica explained, "Sam has no interest in me romantically, but he promised to help me if I killed his wife. He told me that he would arrange for us to be married to make me popular with the media."

"You sicken me!" Jack yelled. "First, you try and have your assassin kill me. Oh, I knew. I outsmarted all of them. I took the president of the security firm and killed him. That's right. I invited him over for a drink. I knew Old Danny Boy wanted me dead, so I killed him and hid his body. That night I put his body in my bed. When your assassin came into my bedroom, he filled Danny Boy full of holes and then set my house on fire. But I was waiting."

"Jack, please..."

"Shut up!" Jack yelled. "Oh, I was waiting," he continued. "I knew Danny Boy's plan. I knew about the fake license, the birth certificate, the whole party, Veronica. Your assassin was going to be me, good old Jack Johnson...good old gullible Jack Johnson. Only I'm not so gullible after all, am I?"

"Jack, please...anything..." Veronica begged.

Jack ignored his wife. "When your assassin drove off in my car, I called the car phone. I gave your little friend the shock of his life. That's when he left town, on my orders, to come here and wait for further instructions. You see, Veronica, I had a hidden camera in the bedroom. I caught him shooting Danny Boy. I also knew about your reservation. Not a bad place, I like it."

"I...oh, Jack, please."

"I came here, Veronica, and I killed him. I injected a heart attack serum into that worthless low-life," Jack finished. "The only problem was, that stupid boy came into the room before I could get my money. My patience was wearing thin, so I killed them. I'll kill that little brat later tonight. That's right, wife of mine, Jack Johnson is in control. What do you think about that?"

"I think you should put your gun down," Hawk yelled, bursting out of the bathroom. Nikki, like a faithful partner, followed behind, aiming her gun at Veronica.

"Don't move," Nikki yelled.

Taken off guard, Jack threw his eyes at Hawk. Unable to control his rage, he aimed his gun at Hawk and tried to fire off a round. Hawk was prepared. Squeezing the trigger, he fired. The bullet screamed across the room and hit Jack in his right wrist. Crying out in pain, Jack dropped his gun and grabbed his wrist. Veronica dashed for the door. Nikki fired her gun, putting a bullet in the door. Veronica froze. "Not bad," Hawk complimented Nikki. Wiping the sweat from his face, he took a deep breath. "Man, you hit a home run with this one, partner."

"A lot of lucky guessing," Nikki confessed. "What do we do now, Hawk? The phones are out."

"First thing's first," Hawk said, marching up to Jack and slinging him down onto the floor. "Who is the assassin? What is his name? I want answers!" he yelled.

"A nobody," Jack yelled back, holding his bleeding wrist, "a loser Danny yanked from prison, just like the rest of us."

"How come I couldn't find any information on him? We found your information."

"Security Level Black," Jack confessed and then threw

his deadly eyes at Veronica. "Security Level Black means an inmate was sentenced to death by the justice system and had no real reason to live. Danny called them his 'moles' because they would do whatever he said. My lovely wife there easily manipulated this guy, not knowing he was sent to kill her as well as me."

"What?" Veronica asked, as the color drained from her face.

"You were dating a psycho," Jack began laughing. "The man's name was Alistair Belton, a man sentenced to death for killing five people. He's better known as the Freeway Killer. You really know how to pick them."

"Shut up!" Veronica screamed, and then she began crying as if she were the victim.

"You're both in hot water," Hawk promised. Glancing at Nikki, he nodded. "We still have a long way to go. Two people are dead, and we have Zach to deal with. The newspaper is going to throw your name all over the place. Your life in town isn't going to be easy for a while. Are you still planning on leaving town?"

"Not on your life," Nikki smiled. "I have too much chocolate to make. Besides, what would you do without me, Hawk?"

Hearing the door creep open, Hawk aimed his gun at the door. Chief Daily appeared, soaking wet from the rain. With his gun drawn, he studied the room. "Power went out in town. I went over to Nikki's cabin. A young lady named Tori told me you two came out to the lodge. I tried calling, but the line was out. Is everything okay?"

"Depends if you still want me to leave," Nikki told Chief Daily.

"If you try, I will arrest you," Chief Daily replied, putting his gun away. "You're still bad luck, but in a good way," he smiled. "Hawk, I need answers. Start talking."

"Nikki will do all the talking, Pop. Right now, we have two dead bodies to retrieve from a cave, along with some money. I'm sure Mr. Johnson here knows where the money is."

Jack Johnson began laughing and didn't stop. "My money," he laughed, "my money, my money…"

Outside the storm raged on.

17

"Here's to Nikki," Hawk said, raising a glass full of chocolate milk.

Sitting in her kitchen with Hawk, Lidia, Tori and Zach, Nikki blushed at all the attention she was receiving. Brushing a few cake crumbs off her yellow dress, she smiled at Hawk. "Hawk is the hero. If he hadn't shot Jack Johnson in the wrist, who knows what would have happened?"

Tori clapped for Hawk. "My hero."

"I was there, too," Zach complained.

"You were in shock." Hawk helped Zach look good in Tori's eyes. "I saw the bodies. I understand what you were feeling, son."

"So what happens now?" Lidia asked, standing up from the kitchen table and refilling her coffee cup. Grateful the case was solved, she felt relaxed enough to ask about Zach's future. "Zach, what will you do?"

Zach looked at Tori. He loved the way she looked in the

blue dress she was wearing. A lot better than the baby t-shirts. "The lodge is mine," he told Tori. "The old man left it to me in his will. Yeah, I know, shocking. I thought maybe I'd stay around, if you want me to."

Tori pointed at the black t-shirt Zach was wearing. "All I want is the real Zach, okay?" she said and gently reached out and held Zach's hand.

Nikki smiled at Lidia. Lidia smiled back. "Well," Hawk said with a belly full of cake, "I think I'm going to go home and sleep twenty-four hours."

"No, you don't," Lidia fussed. "You stay seated. I have an announcement to make that I want everyone to hear. Actually, Nikki and I have an announcement that we want everyone to hear."

Nikki nervously cleared her throat. Leaning against the island stove, she steadied her nerves. "I was offered a job at the paper. I have decided to take the job. In return, I have sold half of the store to Lidia. We are now partners. Also, together, we have decided to fire Tori."

"Fire me?" Tori asked, confused. "I thought you—"

"Young lady," Nikki smiled, "you are going to begin attending college. Lidia and I are going to pay your tuition. There is a nice community college forty minutes south of here."

"Hey now, that's a great idea," Hawk said and clapped for Tori.

"And you," Lidia pointed at Zach, "are going to attend college, too. Now I don't expect you to go full-time because you have a lodge to maintain, but you will go part time."

"Is that what people mean when they say the good guys always win?" Zach asked Tori.

"I think so," Tori smiled happily. "Oh, Ms. Bates…Nikki…Lidia, how can I thank you?"

"By—" Nikki began to speak but paused when the phone hanging beside the refrigerator rang. "Just a second," she said and answered the phone. "Hello…oh, he's here…Hawk, it's Chief Daily."

Hawk stood up, stretched his arms, and walked to the phone. "Yeah Pop…What?…You're putting me on. When?…Okay, I'll be right over." Hawk handed the phone back to Nikki. "Nikki, grab your purse, we have another homicide."

"What?" Nikki gasped.

"Millins Gas Station. A woman was found dead in her car," Hawk said and threw his hands up into the air. "I'm not saying a word, okay? Pop was the one who called you bad luck over the phone."

"Remind me to slug him later," Nikki told Hawk. "Lidia, Tori, Zach, wash up for me, please. I'll probably be late getting home."

Lidia walked to the kitchen table and sat down. "Tori, honey," she said, "maybe you should begin carrying some four-leaf clovers around and…sure, why not, add in some rabbits' feet just in case."

Nikki rolled her eyes. "Very funny, Lidia."

Lidia laughed. "Oh, honey, go and solve another case. We're here if you need us, and you probably will. I told Herbert just yesterday that I had a feeling the rest I was getting was only temporary."

Nikki quickly hugged Lidia and Tori. "Another chocolate-covered mystery," she said and winked at Hawk. "Okay, let's go."

Hawk hesitated. "Wait a minute," he said, "where's your gun?"

"I don't—"

"Go get it," Hawk ordered Nikki. "From now on, when you're with me, you're carrying heat."

Lidia noticed that Hawk spoke to Nikki the way a husband speaks to his wife. She expected Nikki to argue back, but instead, she saw Nikki look at Hawk in a very peculiar manner. "Yes, dear," Nikki said and walked out of the kitchen toward her bedroom. Maybe, Lidia thought, taking a sip of her coffee, her dear Nikki was beginning to allow Hawk into her heart. Slowly, of course, the way anyone would. But slow was better than no movement at all. In time, Nikki just might be able to allow Hawk to completely enter her heart. But what would that mean? Could Hawk handle a woman who was fearless in the face of danger? Raising her eyes, she studied Hawk staring after Nikki. According to the look in his eyes, Lidia guessed that Hawk could not only deal with Nikki, but was anxious to prove how much they belonged together. But, Lidia saw, Hawk was a patient man who knew how to wait for the best chocolate-covered kiss in town.

"And don't shoot yourself in the foot," Hawk yelled after Nikki.

Well, Lidia laughed to herself, maybe.

ABOUT THE AUTHOR

Wendy Meadows is the USA Today bestselling author of many novels and novellas, from cozy mysteries to clean, sweet romances. Check out her popular cozy mystery series Sweetfern Harbor, Alaska Cozy and Sweet Peach Bakery, just to name a few.

If you enjoyed this book, please take a few minutes to leave a review. Authors truly appreciate this, and it helps other readers decide if the book might be for them. Thank you!

Get in touch with Wendy
www.wendymeadows.com

- amazon.com/author/wendymeadows
- goodreads.com/wendymeadows
- bookbub.com/authors/wendy-meadows
- facebook.com/AuthorWendyMeadows
- twitter.com/wmeadowscozy

Copyright © 2017 by Wendy Meadows

All rights reserved.

No part of this publication may be reproduced, distributed or transmitted in any form or by any means, without prior written permission.

This is a work of fiction. Names, characters, places, and incidents are a product of the author's imagination. Locales and public names are sometimes used for atmospheric purposes. Any resemblance to actual people, living or dead, or to businesses, companies, events, institutions, or locales is completely coincidental.

Printed in the United States of America

Printed in Great Britain
by Amazon